OTHER BOOKS IN PRINT
By Lloyd Wright

"BACK THEN UNTIL NOW"

"POEMS AND THOUGHTS"

"GRAMP'S CHRISTMAS TALES"

"STORIES FOR GRAMPS LITTLE FRIENDS"

"MORE STORIES FOR GRAMPS LITTLE FRIENDS"

"GRAMPS SHORT AND TALL TALES"

"DONNA, DONNIE AND LITTLE SAD WEE WILLY"

"GRAMPS VARIETY OF STORIES"

"BROKEN CRAYONS AND SAND IN THEIR SHOES"

E-MAIL
lmwright2301@yahoo.com

Kindergarten Tales
And Then Some

LLOYD WRIGHT

iUniverse, Inc.
Bloomington

Kindergarten Tales And Then Some

Copyright © 2011 Lloyd Wright

iUniverse books may be ordered through booksellers or by contacting:

iUniverse
1663 Liberty Drive
Bloomington, IN 47403
www.iuniverse.com
1-800-Authors (1-800-288-4677)

ISBN: 978-1-4620-0153-8 (pbk)
ISBN: 978-1-4620-0154-5 (cloth)
ISBN: 978-1-4620-0155-2 (ebk)

Printed in the United States of America

iUniverse rev. date: 3/1/2011

DEDICATION

This book is dedicated to my wife, children, grandchildren and great grandchildren.

PICTURE ON THE BACK COVER

The picture on the back cover is my great granddaughter Charlee Beth and myself in the garden.

A VERY SPECIAL THANK YOU

Jan and Wayne Fuller have again assisted me tremendously by proof reading my stories and setting the book up. I have read all of Wayne's published books and have enjoyed all of them.

ABOUT THE BOOK

Kindergarten Tales and Then Some takes you to school and even the North Pole. It is about riding a school bus and should show the children going on their first bus ride there is nothing to fear. The story on school supplies was written to show what is required now. When I entered my first year of school back when, I only needed a Big Chief tablet, lead pencil, and a box of crayons. It tells about holidays and how they celebrate them in kindergarten. Santa Claus is involved with his reindeer and sleigh at Christmas time. Throughout the book you will find children's compassion for others.

Contents

Bernie The School Bus 2
Kindergarten School Supplies For Gabby 12
Clay 16
Will They Remember Me 20
Best Friends 24
Melvin Always Wore A Hat 30
The Kitchen Broom 38
Santa And The Grand Canyon 44
Old Man Halters 52
A Special Turkey 60
Gifts To Give 66
The Doll In The Window 72
Faded Plastic Flowers 80
Santa Claus And Little Toot 84
Christmas Tree In A Window 100
She Always Wore House Slippers 106
I Heard Animals Singing 110
Arkansas Red Cedar Tree 116
Mrs. Hopper Visits Kindergarten 122
A Date To Remember 128
A Very Special Key 132
Mrs. Finch's Annual Christmas Program 136
When The Spring Flowers Bloom 142
Johnny Is Going Nowhere 150

Bernie The School Bus

WRITTEN BY
LLOYD WRIGHT

Bernie The School Bus

Little Bernie sits anxiously in the school bus garage waiting for the final inspection. This will be his first year with a route to pick up the children for school. He wants all the children to like him and treat him kindly just like they would like to be treated. His mother, Nurse Bernice, is the special needs bus and has been for several years. Bernie's father is the large diesel powered bus. He has the longest route and can carry the most children. He also is used to transport the children to all sporting activities and out of town school trips. Little Bernie loves to hear the sound his father makes when he starts his trips. Bernie does not like the smell of the smoke his father leaves behind but yet he hopes to someday be just like him. His mother complains to his father about his smoking to no avail. She knows it is just the diesel he uses and not a bad habit.

Little Bernie did not have to wait long for the school bus mechanic. The mechanic checked him from headlights to taillights. He raised his hood and checked the level of his oil and coolant. He was ever so gentle with Bernie and talked to him as he checked him inside and out. He checked every tire for the correct air pressure and made sure all the lug nuts were secure. He checked all the safety features and especially the lights. When Bernie's inspection was through in the garage, the mechanic started Bernie and parked him outside. The lady assigned to drive Bernie is new to the job as a bus driver and unfamiliar with the assigned bus route she and Bernie must travel every school day come rain or shine. The bus driver had requested a familiarization ride, which had been approved and was to take place this very day.

Bernie was day dreaming in the warm August sun when he became aware of a short lady with gray hair and a soft gentle voice approaching him with a person he had seen driving other buses. Bernie listened as the experienced bus driver told and showed the lady what she must check every morning before picking up the children. They opened his door and climbed the steps leading up inside. The newly assigned bus driver sat down in the driver's seat and the person assigned to show her the bus route sat in the front seat next to the door. Bernie soon found out the pleasant lady assigned to drive him was named Annie. She is retired and is a grandparent to school age children just like the children they would be carrying to school. She had time to spare plus she did need to supplement her retirement check.

She adjusted the mirrors and when all the necessary preparations were through, she started Bernie's engine. Bernie was so anxious to please Annie that he started immediately and purred like a kitten. She put Bernie in gear and they slowly departed the school bus yard. She turned on the turn signals to show which way they were going to turn on the main road leaving the school. Bernie winked his turn signal lights just like he had been asked. This was all strange territory for Bernie and he was cautious as they started the bus route he would soon become so familiar with. As they rode through the residential neighborhoods, he smiled when he saw children playing in their front yards and waving at him. He listened ever so intently as the bus driver trainer told Annie where to go and where each stop would be. Before every stop he must turn on his flashing warning signals and then extend the arm in front after he stopped to protect his precious cargo as they get on or off. After they had finished the bus route Annie drove Bernie back to the school bus yard and parked him. The next time they left the school bus yard would be the first day of school.

Bernie sat under a hot August sun for what seemed to him an eternity. Record temperatures were being set and he thought the first day of school would never arrive. One morning as he sat under the early morning sun, he saw Annie along with a host of other drivers enter the bus parking lot. Annie quickly but thoroughly made her inspection of Bernie and then opened Bernie's door and climbed the steps. Annie did have a little difficulty climbing the steps and she then realized the younger children, especially the children in kindergarten, would struggle with their backpacks getting on and off Bernie. Annie adjusted the driver's seat and double checked the mirrors. She then turned on Bernie's ignition and started Bernie's engine. The first day of school had arrived, nineteen August two thousand and ten.

Annie and Bernie were each nervous in their own way as they left the school bus parking lot and started their assigned route. They soon were approaching the first stop. Bernie saw a little boy with a backpack on his back and his arms wrapped around his mother's leg. She held a young girl in her arms. An old dog was sitting beside them wagging his tail. Bernie proudly flashed his lights that Annie had turned on. They came to a stop next to the tearful kindergarten passenger. Annie extended Bernie's arm in front and opened the door. The young new student was sobbing and would not turn loose of his mother's leg. The boy sobbed to his mother that his dog would miss him. After much gentle persuasion, the little kindergarten boy was struggling up Bernie's steps with his mother's help. The dog just sat and watched. It did lick the boy good-by. With tears flowing from both the mother and young lad, Annie closed the door and slowly pulled away. Bernie could feel the boy's face wet with tears pressed against his window. Bernie witnessed this scene at several stops. It made him sad and as he listened to those that were crying and they were no comfort for the other children crying. The older students tried to calm them down but to no avail. When the route was completed Annie and Bernie returned to the school where the children would get off Bernie to start their first day of school. Bernie was proud of his students. He would soon get to know each and everyone of his passengers before the school year had been in session for a month.

When Annie and Bernie returned to pick up their students that first afternoon, they found those which had been crying earlier in the day now had smiles on their faces. The clean clothes they had wore to school showed signs of tear stains and playground dirt. Some shoes were untied and hair uncombed. Bernie smiled when he saw them. At each stop, where the younger children lived, a parent or grandparent was waiting and the students departed out the door faster than they had entered that morning. Each day as school progressed, the route got easier for Annie and Bernie. There still was tears but not as many. Bernie noticed some of the students even would run to the bus stop as their mother stood in the doorway shouting last minute instruction or good-bys.

Annie proved to be a very caring bus driver. If it was raining she always tried to stop away from a water hole. As a grandmother, she knew that water holes attracted children and made them jump in them. She always cautioned them to stay out of the puddles. She quickly learned to glance at each departing passenger to see if they had their backpacks and coats. This saved her time when she checked the bus and would find nothing left behind. If there was something left then she would have to turn it in for the parent or student to claim. This also helped insure that necessary home work would not be forgotten or school work taken home to show to the parents. Bernie loved to hear Annie greet every student in the mornings. She was gentle but firm with her passengers. She knew if discipline was not maintained then innocent students would suffer and safety would be jeopardized. She was also aware that any rowdy behavior, if left unchecked, could hurt Bernie.

Annie would talk to Bernie as a friend when alone. Annie and Bernie would watch to see what the children were carrying to and from school. As they drove along their route one day, they noticed witches, ghost and goblins in the yards and on the front porches. Annie explained to Bernie that Halloween was coming and Autumn colors were everywhere. Bernie would listen as Annie spoke to each kindergarten student and praise them for the nice work they did on their Halloween paperwork. They did dress as ghosts and goblins and try to scare each other. On the day of their school Halloween party, they each carried a plastic jack-o-lantern with treats inside home. When they returned to the school bus parking lot, not a single jack-o-lantern or treat could be found when Annie checked Bernie for forgotten items inside.

November was a pretty fall month. The air was cool in the morning and sweaters and coats were worn in the morning and at least one was left on the bus in the afternoon daily. Some mornings frost was on Bernie's windshield and the defroster had to run for a while before they could leave the school grounds. One morning it was so heavy it had to be removed using spray. Annie loved to watch the colorful leaves dance as they fell through the air to the ground. She described it to Bernie as the autumn leave ballet. Bernie saw papers with a turkey colored in the children's hand and in the see through backpacks when they left school. He heard them talking about the class Thanksgiving program they were practicing for every day at school. Bernie smiled when he saw the kindergarten boys and girls wearing pilgrim clothes the day of their play. He knew that school can be fun while the children learn. As the days got cooler and shorter Annie found coats and hats less frequent when she checked Bernie each school day.

Thanksgiving was soon over and the month of December began. The yards and houses were now starting to have Christmas decorations. Bernie listened as Annie would start each day humming a Christmas carol as she checked him. She would sing after they left the school ground until they came to their first stop. She would greet each student with a happy greeting as they boarded the bus. The struggle up and down the steps for the kindergarteners became less difficult with each school day. As Christmas approached the children were growing more excited. Some even practiced singing carols for their class Christmas play as they rode home. The air was cold enough that the windows would steam up when the children blew their breath on them. It would quickly disappear as they wiped it off or would draw pictures in it with their finger tips.

Bernie knew Christmas must be Annie's favorite holiday. They loved to see the children dressed in their bright clothes. Santa Claus hats were worn by many of the students. Annie even wore a Santa hat. Bernie woke up one morning covered with a light coat of snow. He did not know what it was until Annie explained it to him. It made everyone get in the Christmas spirit. The children did complain because it did not snow enough to cancel school. The last week of school before Christmas the children carried presents to school to exchange and to give to the foster children. Christmas trees were in every window and some roof tops decorated with Christmas decorations. Bernie's favorite was a Santa sleigh with eight reindeer. One of the reindeer was Rudolph.

Bernie was surprised and very proud when he was chosen to carry two kindergarten classes to deliver their Christmas presents to the foster children. Annie drove Bernie since they were a team. Annie sang Christmas carols with the children as they traveled to deliver the presents. As each child carried their present into the bank lobby where the presents were being collected, the children voices all joined together in song. Annie had to wipe tears from her eyes. It made her so proud to see the children give their gifts so unselfishly.

Bernie was sad when the last school day came. Now he would have to stay in the school bus yard for two weeks while the children were on Christmas vacation. Bernie would sure miss Annie's tender touch and gentle voice. Annie had made a small wreath and hung on Bernie's dash. He was very proud of it. Maybe, just maybe his mom and dad had a Christmas present for him. He was sure Santa would bring him one. He had heard the children say he would not miss anybody. Christmas Eve Bernie would be watching the sky for Santa Claus and his reindeer.

It was snowing ever so slightly the day before Christmas. The snow stopped at noon and the sky cleared a bright crispy blue. After the sunset, the moon lit up the sky and all the stars twinkled brightly. One star in the eastern sky shined brighter than all the rest. Bernie was watching the star and it seemed to beckon him just like it had the shepherds and three wise men. As Bernie was intently watching the star in the east, he heard bells softly ringing in the clear crispy sky. As he searched the sky to see where it was coming from he saw eight reindeer pulling a sleigh full of presents passing between him and the bright moon. He knew it was Santa Claus just like his mother and Annie had told him. He closed his headlights and pretended to be sound asleep so Santa would stop by. Santa did land in the school bus yard and left Bernie three presents.

Bernie could hardly wait to open his Christmas gifts. He could not imagine what Santa could bring him useful since he was just a little school bus. As soon as the cold morning sun reflected on Bernie's frosty windshield, he anxiously opened his presents. The first present was a pretty red throw blanket, which he had asked for so Annie could place it on the cold drivers seat on cold mornings. The next present was a windshield scraper with gloves for Annie to use to clean the frost off of his windshield. The third present was large and when Bernie opened it he found a set of tire chains to help him safely through the snow on his school route. Yes, Santa is real and remembered Bernie. It was a perfect ending to the first half of the school year. Now Bernie must wait for the New Year and school to start again.

The new year arrived cold and snowy. Bernie did not mind the snow since he would get to pick up his school friends and start the bus route with Annie. When Bernie and Annie picked up the children on the first day school was back in session they noticed the children had been busy during Christmas vacation making snowmen. They also noticed little footprints all over every front yard. Bernie was so happy to be back to work. He had missed Annie and his school friends. Annie did find a few mittens left after they returned to the bus schoolyard but no coats when she checked Bernie each school day.

January passed quickly with no missed school for snow days. February arrived with cold weather and more snow. School was let out early the first Friday due to a snow storm. The week of Valentine's Day, Annie received several cards from the students. She read them to Bernie at the end of their bus route each day. Bernie was so proud of the students for remembering Annie. February passed quickly and spring was soon in the air. Bernie noticed during the month of March, flowers starting to bloom and grass was turning the yards green. Spring break arrived and Bernie sat in the school bus yard for a week. He sure missed Annie and the children.

When school resumed, Bernie and Annie noticed how all the yards were brilliant with color. Spring flowers were in full bloom and all the trees were getting their new leaves. The children were all rosy cheeked when they climbed onto Bernie each morning. The air was cool enough to make them wear sweaters. This meant Annie would be finding sweaters left behind to turn in to the lost and found. Annie and Bernie enjoyed the Easter season but missed the children when they were off for the holiday. After Easter, Bernie caught a glimpse of an occasional colored Easter egg hiding in the grass or flower beds. He even spotted one hiding in a tree.

The Spring months passed too quickly for Annie and Bernie. The month of May appeared out of nowhere. This meant the school year was almost over. Bernie had enjoyed the children and all the sights he had seen. He would especially miss Annie when school was out for the summer. When the kindergarteners graduated as well as the seniors, Bernie also received praise for completing his first year of school as a school bus. Annie was very proud of Bernie and told him as such. She also informed him she would be with him when the next school year started. He had learned so much from Annie and had experienced so much. In a way he was like the kindergarten students and was ready for his upcoming second year of school.

Kindergarten School Supplies For Gabby

Written By
Lloyd Wright

Kindergarten School Supplies For Gabby

Gabby was looking forward to the day she started kindergarten. Now Gabby is her nickname but her true name is Gabriela Sosa. She likes the name Gabby and hoped her kindergarten teacher would call her by her nickname. Gabby's mother "Christie," had picked up a list of needed school supplies the week before. Gabby wanted to go shopping with her mother to pick out the supplies. Gabby asked to see the list of supplies and her mother let her look at it. She could not read but could see it was a whole page. She asked her mother to read it to her. She read it as follows.

KINDERGARTEN
2010-2011

Supply list
(1) Box of 24 regular Crayola crayons - basic colors
(no Roseart crayons or jumbo)
Scissors - Fiskar brand (left handed for lefties)
(1) 4 oz. Elmer's glue
(2) Large glue sticks
(1) pkg. Regular #2 pencils
(1) Primary tablet with dotted lines. Example shown

_____

- -

_____

(1) Liquid soap or Germ X

(2) Large box of Kleenex

(1) Prang or Crayola water paints

(1) Plastic supply box with lid attached. Example
Spacemaker - standard 8 ¼" x 5 ¼"

(1) Large box of baby wipes(1) Old paint shirt (dad's old t-shirt)

(1) MESH OR CLEAR BACKPACK ONLY!

PLEASE PLACE CHILD'S NAME ON EVERYTHING.

The day to go shopping for school supplies had finally arrived. Gabby woke up early and didn't even take time to rub her eyes. Gabby had been looking forward to this day for such a long time and finally it was here. Gabby knew her brother Griffin was in pre-school and would also need school supplies but not like the ones she would be picking out for kindergarten class. She did not mind that her brother was going shopping with her mother and her but she did not want to wait all day for him to get up and get dressed. Gabby and her brother were the best of friend and enjoyed sharing as brothers and sisters should. Gabby did inform Griffin that her supplies would be for kindergarten and not pre-school.

Gabby was sitting at the breakfast table waiting for her brother. She wanted to go shopping as soon as they had eaten their breakfast. She knew what store they would be shopping at and she also knew all her friends were getting their supplies there. She was worried they would run out of supplies and then she would not have them for the first day of school. Christie kept assuring her daughter there would be plenty of supplies and if not at that store they could go elsewhere.

The time finally came to go shopping after what seemed like an eternity to Gabby. She was all bubbly as well as her brother. When they finally arrived at the store, the parking lot was busy and this worried Gabby they may not find a parking spot. Lady luck was with them as they saw a vehicle backing out close to the front door. They waited and when it finished backing out, they pulled into the vacant spot. Gabby breathed a sigh of relief. Now she hoped the store still had plenty of school supplies left. The busy parking lot concerned her. She had her seat belt off and was ready to jump out as soon as her mother opened the door for them. Gabby and her brother held onto their mother's hands and quickly guided her to where the shopping carts were waiting. The first one Christie picked out wanted to go its own direction so she put it back and picked out another one. This one was better although it kind of had a bounce in one front wheel.

Gabby helped her mother push the cart over to the school supply aisle. When they turned into the aisle Gabby was relieved to see the shelves were still well stocked. Gabby picked up the supplies as her mother guided the shopping cart down the aisle and read the list she had brought along.

The hardest decision Gabby had to make was picking out her backpack. It had to be very special. She finally found the one that had caught her attention. It was perfect and when her mother looked at it, she saw it had "Gabby," written all over it.

They had to go to another aisle to find a large box of baby wipes, liquid soap or Germ X, and a box of Kleenex. They had found every item needed on the list except an old t-shirt which she already knew which one she would take to school to protect her school clothes when she painted. They had also found all of the items Griffin would need. When they arrived at the check-out counter, Gabby put all her supplies on the belt to be rang up and Griffin did the same with his. They both had been a great help to their mother.

Gabby and Griffin helped their mother put the school supplies in the vehicle. When they were all strapped in, there was one more stop they wanted their mother to make. It had to do with growling tummies. They knew just the place to go and knew they could help their mother find it. Gabby was ready for kindergarten and now it was time to celebrate.

Clay

WRITTEN BY
LLOYD WRIGHT

Clay

A man called "Gramps", listened intently one morning as he heard a gentleman talk about his days in school and his memory of a certain Art teacher. The Art teacher started out the art session this particular day by taking some clay and placing it on a wheel. She took some more clay and placed on another wheel for a student. As her wheel turned she took her hands and started to form a sculpture as the student followed her example. The other students in the class watched as the teacher worked and formed a beautiful piece of art. The student followed the teacher's instruction but her work of art could not match the teacher's skilled hands. The students were so involved they did not notice how fast the art class was over until the bell alerted them. When the bell rang the teacher took her hands and collapsed the beautiful piece of art back into a glob of clay as she informed her students they would demonstrate how to form something else from the clay tomorrow. This one student could not believe she had destroyed such a beautiful piece of sculpture.

As Gramps listened to this story he thought of the kindergarten students he reads to every week. The clay reminded him of the kindergarten students and the their teachers are the art instructor. The kindergarten teacher can take these children and form them into fine individuals that no pottery could match. Everyday they are molded further though learning. Once they learn how to read the world of knowledge is opened up to them and what they are capable of learning is unlimited. They are taught numbers and how to add and subtract.

They are taught there are four seasons and how mother nature decorates each one different. As they learn the different colors they can see them as the seasons change just like a canvas changes colors with each stoke of a paint brush. Each student is required to bring to school and old shirt to be used when they use their water colors. The pictures they learn to paint and the overflow of the paint on their hands and wiped on the shirt from painting is also a work of art. It will show hand prints and odd shaped designs.

During the fall a teacher took her class to a nearby yard where they gathered different pieces of mother nature which lay on the ground. They gathered little rocks, twigs, colored leaves, acorns, and anything that caught their eye. When they returned to the classroom each student glued their own collection onto a piece of paper. When the glue was dry and all secure they took it home to their parents. Some parents bragged on this work of art while others threw it in the trash. This crushed the child just like the art teacher had done with the piece of pottery she had collapsed for use another day.

As the kindergarteners learned their colors they used crayons and paints on different assignments the teacher gives to them. When they are finished the teacher would grade and send this master piece home with each student. Some end up being proudly displayed on refrigerator doors and some are thrown indifferent into the trash. Again some of the work of kindergarten art is destroyed by this thoughtless action and part of what the teacher has been molding from this kindergarten clay is being crushed.

Pictures they made for each holiday were colored or painted and proudly displayed on a wall in the classroom. When the holiday arrived, each student carried their prized work of art home. Again some were put on the refrigerator door or proudly sent to grandparents. Some are again thoughtlessly discarded in the trash without even being viewed by the parents. These parents are doing to the child the same thing the art teacher had done to the beautiful piece of pottery. They are undoing what the kindergarten teacher has been molding with their child.

Parents who do not encourage and help their school age children do not seem to realize how they are tearing apart the most precious gift they will ever receive. Their lack of interest may be from using drugs or self interest. If the parents use drugs then the children would assume it would be alright for them to try and use them. Drugs will not only take away the ability the students have to be shaped by teachers through learning but could also destroy this great piece of art which has been especially made for the parents.

Gramps believes each child is like a piece of clay waiting to be shaped and formed by a caring teacher who is the potter, and a good home life.

Will They Remember Me

Written By
Lloyd Wright

Will They Remember Me

Gramps is a volunteer who has read to kindergarten classes for several years. He never attended or graduated from kindergarten because the school he attended did not have kindergarten. He started elementary school in the first grade so therefore he has never graduated from kindergarten. The reason he has read to kindergarten classes for several years is because the teachers will not graduate him on to the first grade. Every year as his kindergarten classmates graduate they ask Gramps if he will read to them the next year in the first grade. The teacher explains to them that Gramps has again failed kindergarten so therefore must return to kindergarten the following school year.

Gramps returns the following school year and low and behold is immediately informed he probably won't pass again for a multitude of reasons. They tell him he has retention deficient, misses too many school days each year, plays with puppets when he should be reading, and last but not least he not only reads to the children but tells them untrue tales. His favorite holiday is Christmas and he believes in Santa. He wears hearing aids and tells the students, when asked about them, that they are radios he communicates to Santa with daily. He also rides his pretend Shetland pony to school. When he is late he blames it on the pony. Some of the students even have looked out of the class room window and saw the pony. Gramps is beginning to think that maybe, just maybe it is not him but it is the teachers not doing a satisfactory job of teaching. When he tells them as such they just give him a disgusted look and kind of huff like the Big Bad Wolf.

One question he hears from his kindergarten teachers at graduation time is.

"Will they remember me?"

Gramps always assures them.

" Yes, they will remember you".

He remembers his first teacher, "Miss Taylor," who was a kind and friendly teacher. Gramps then recalls a teacher he had for the third and fourth grade. She left a very, very, very lasting impression on him. He has told all his children, grandchildren, and great grandchildren about Miss Mierberg. She not only left a lasting impression on him, but a few lumps. When he looks at the arthritis in his knuckles he recalls how she would sneak up behind and crack him across the knuckles with the edge of a ruler that had a metal piece running the length of it. She would also grab him by his collar and slam him in a corner of the class room and make him face the corner until she told him he could return to his desk. She was great at suddenly appearing out of no where behind his back and pop him on the back of his head so his head would bounce back and forth between the corner walls thus making him hit the wall two or three times. She also was excellent at lining up Gramps and his male classmates and walking down the row of boys and slapping each one on the cheeks. Yes, vengeance was hers daily. She believed in teaching like the song says.

"Reading, writing, and arithmetic, taught to the tune of the hickory stick."

Sometimes the children would get wet from the weather or from playing outside on the playground. It was never too hot or too cold to go out for recess. Wet clothes and cold weather do not make a great combination. Miss Meirberg did not care if you shivered yourself to death. She would just say.

"Maybe someday you will learn not to get wet."

She never taught us how to stop the rain or snow or how to keep the ice from melting on the playground under the swings or slide. Sometimes she would let the girls stand by the heater to get warm or to dry their clothes but not the boys. What I did learn from her was how to shiver and get frozen feet.

One of Gramps best friends in Miss Mierberg's class had a glass eye. Miss Mierberg slapped this boy on the back of the head one day as he was getting a drink of water and knocked his glass eye out. Gramps recalls to this day watching it roll around. She had to wash it off and put it back in his eye socket. Sometimes the eye would move and look at his nose or his ear. Miss Meirberg didn't care and left it like that. When he was in Miss Taylor's room she would straighten it where it looked forward. Yes, he remembered Miss Mierberg all his life. It was not for good reasons but strictly from fear.

To this very day when Gramps meets a new teacher or a substitute, he is in constant fear the teacher will be a Miss Mierberg. If it ever is, he will quit his kindergarten education because he would be assured of not graduating because fear would keep him from learning. He does not think his heart is in good enough shape to tolerate another teacher like Miss Mierberg. He is so thankful he has not found another teacher like her. She put fear in him that was imbedded for life. She did give him an education that would last a life time.

His first grade teacher is remembered for the great teacher and kind lady she was. One thing she did teach Gramps was he did not have to fear all teachers. Also because of Miss Taylor, he can tell his kindergarten teachers with confidence that all their students will remember them for the rest of their lives, because they all are caring teachers and have become a major part of their kindergarten students lives. They are the ones who cared for their welfare and cracked the door open to their abilities to read and learn.

They will not be remembered as a Miss Mierberg. Those days are gone and Gramps hopes they are gone forever! She still lurks in his mind though, which makes him be constantly on the lookout for her.

Best Friends

WRITTEN BY
LLOYD WRIGHT

Best Friends

Megan and Donna are best friends and have been since they first met. When Megan went outside to ride her little tricycle, Donna would be there to get a ride standing up behind Megan. Megan sure liked her best friend and did most of the talking. As she slowly rode her tricycle on the sidewalk in front of her home she would continuously talk to her best friend. It seemed like she played with Donna more than she played with her younger sister. She always gave the same short answer when her mother would ask her.

"Who were you talking to Megan?"

Megan would reply.

" Donna."

One day Megan and Donna were playing house in the playhouse when they heard a knock on the door. It was Megan's mother with cookies and a cold drink. Along with her was Jenny, Megan's younger sister. Megan and Donna sat the little playhouse table and they had a nice afternoon tea party together. They sat and visited for awhile until the goodies and drink were gone. Megan's mother gathered up the drink cups and went back to the house with a soft smile on her face. She was pleased to see both her daughters treated Donna so nicely. Donna was at their home so much she was like a member of the family.

One afternoon Megan and Donna were riding the tricycle together when Megan spotted a bug on the sidewalk. She stopped and pointed the bug out to Donna. Jenny and her Grandpa were visiting as they sat on the front steps watching Megan and her friend. Jenny just had to walk over and see what her sister and her sister's friend were looking at on the sidewalk with so much interest. When she arrived over to see what was on the sidewalk, she saw it was just a little bug crawling around. She quickly informed her sister it was just a bug as she smashed it with her foot. Needless to say, it was not appreciated what Jenny had done and Megan quickly told her so. Donna just watched and never said a word.

That very same afternoon, Megan and Jenny were looking at a potato bug as it crawled in the yard by the garage. Of course Donna was their also with Megan. Megan asked her dad about the potato bug and what it did. He quickly informed the girls the bug is where potatoes came from. That made a lot of sense to the girls. Megan and Donna made sure Jenny did not send that little bug to where ever they go when they are smashed. The bug needed protected if they wanted any more French fries or potato chips.

Grandpa was visiting for a few days during this time and enjoyed going for a walk with the girls everyday. Along the sidewalk where they walked was a low hanging tree branch with a used vacant bird's nest. Grandpa knew it was empty and the girls wanted to look in it. He sneaked back and put some small round rocks in the nest. The next day the girls pleaded to look in the nest so he lift them up one by one and let they see the rock eggs, They of course wanted to know what kind of eggs were in the nest. Grandpa replied.

"Those are rock eggs laid by rock birds."

Everyday that nest was checked while grandpa was on vacation. When he left, the girls asked their dad daily to take them to check the rock bird nest. Grandpa figured if their dad could tell them about potato bugs and where potatoes came from, then their dad could tell them about rock birds and explain why they never hatch.

Everyday they had to check the nest to see it they had hatched.

One week-end the family traveled to Fish Lake. It is their favorite place to relax and enjoy the week-end as a family. Of course Donna also went with them. Megan had asked her to come along. When she is not with Megan she missed her. They arrived in the evening and had time to relax and snack before bedtime. Early the next morning Megan and her best friend were standing outside enjoying the scenery. They heard the front door open to the cabin. They saw Megan's mother step outside to enjoy the fresh air with the girls. Jenny was right behind her peeking out of the screen door. Megan heard her mother ask.

"Where are you Megan?"

Megan replied.

"I am right here mom."

Again Megan's mother asked.

"Where are you Megan?"

Again Megan replied.

"I am right here mom."

This time her mother asked.

"No Megan, I mean where are you at."

This time Megan pointed at herself as she firmly said.

"Momma, I am right her!"

Megan's mother smiled as she replied.

"Yes Megan you are right here, but I meant for you to answer Fish Lake."

Donna even got to spend nights at Megan's house. They would play games and then take their bath together. Megan was always proud to show Donna her pajamas. These two proved that nothing will ever come between best friends. They even let Jenny play games with them and shared toys. All holidays were spent together. Donna was like a sister to Megan and a member of the family. Where ever Megan went, so did Donna. They saw movies together, took vacations together with Megan's mom and dad, and even went to Disneyland.

One day Megan's mom told her they had to go shopping for school supplies. The time had come for Megan to go to kindergarten. Donna and Jenny went along on the shopping trip. All the supplies were bought that day along with a stop at their favorite store, which sold hamburgers, French fries, and ice cream. Megan talked non stop to Donna about school. Megan knew she would be going to school with her best friend.

Megan's mother took them to school the first day and was introduced to the teacher. Megan was shown her desk with her name tag on it. Donna was in the same class. Megan was not too anxious to meet all her new classmates. She would talk to Donna until the teacher would intervene. When it was time for lunch, Donna and Megan sat at the same table and shared their meal. After lunch it was time for recess and go to the playground. Megan would only play with Donna. They played on the slide and the jungle gym. The teacher was concerned about Megan. She was consistently distracted by a girl called Donna. Donna was the only one Megan wanted to sit by in the classroom and the lunch room. Donna was the only one she would play with on the playground. If this distraction continued, the teacher knew Megan would fall behind the other students in learning.

After one week of school had finished, the kindergarten teacher wrote the following note to Megan's parents.

To: Megan's parents.

It seems that Megan is more interested in being with her best friend Donna than school. As you and I know, Donna is her imaginary friend and is not enrolled in school. Somehow it needs to be explained to Megan that Donna can not attend anymore kindergarten classes.
Thank you
Mrs. Taylor, Megan's kindergarten teacher

P.S. I am a parent to a young girl and understand about best friends.

Melvin Always Wore A Hat

WRITTEN BY
LLOYD WRIGHT

Melvin Always Wore A Hat

Melvin's mother put a hat on her new born son's bald head while in the hospital and insured he had one on when they went home from the hospital. He received three more hats when his mother's friends welcomed them home. He now had a little red hat, blue hat, and a green hat. Melvin wore a hat twenty four hours a day except when he took his bath. He had several little night hats and his mother put one on him whenever he took a nap. She did not want his head or ears to get cold. When his night hat came off in the morning, it was replaced with his play hat. Melvin was so accustomed to wearing a hat that he never tried to remove it. When his mother put a hat on him it stayed there until she removed it. She always made sure his hat did not bend his ears down because she didn't want his ears to stick out when he was older.

Melvin's dad bought him a camouflage hat the first fall of Melvin's life. Melvin loved the hat very much and even wore it to bed. He did not want to take it off when it came bath time. The only thing which made him give up wearing his camouflage hat was when the Christmas season came and he was given a red stocking hat like Santa. He spent the month of December sitting under the Christmas tree looking at his reflection in a silver Christmas ornament. The tree fascinated him so much he never tried to remove any of its decorations. When presents started to appear, a special space under the tree was saved for Melvin. His mother bought him an elf outfit to wear, which he wore with his Santa Claus stocking hat. He appeared to be part of the Christmas tree decoration at first glance.

Melvin protested loudly when Christmas was over and the Christmas tree decorations were removed from the tree and the tree was taken down and stored. He continued to wear his Santa Claus hat though. His dad finally convinced him to have it removed when he gave him a little hunting hat with deer horns on it. Melvin would sit in front of the full length mirror in the hallway and look at himself. It did give him a better reflection than the Christmas tree bulb. When he put his face close to the Christmas bulb, his face looked bigger when he was close to it. When he put his face close to the mirror, his face never changed like it did in the bulb.

Melvin gave up his deer horn hat for a hat with Easter bunny ears on it. He loved the ears except when his little puppy would try to attack the ears, then Melvin would giggle and try to get away. His bunny hat did keep his ears warm when he went outside. Melvin loved his hat with the ears and wore it all the time. The puppy did manage to pull a sneak attack one day and get Melvin's hat off his head. It disappeared down the hallway carrying the Easter Bunny hat with the long ears flopping. By the time Melvin had alerted his mother about the hat, one ear had been chewed off. Melvin didn't seem to care though as he wore it daily for a week before his dad bought him a new baseball hat. With a sigh Melvin traded his one eared hat for the new baseball hat.

Melvin was soon very proud of his baseball hat. He would study it in the hallway mirror as he wrinkled his nose. He had learned how to wrinkle his nose from his dad. When his dad held him in the evening he would make funny faces to make Melvin laugh. Melvin caught on how to wrinkle his nose and practiced it every day. He could see his little hat move when he wrinkled his nose in front of the mirror. One day as he was watching himself in the mirror, his puppy pulled another sneak attack and got his baseball hat. He alerted his mom to the attack and she quickly retrieved his hat with just a few puppy teeth marks on it.

Melvin's mother had a birthday party for his first birthday. Melvin wore a little party birthday hat during the party but traded it immediately after the party was over for his new cowboy hat he had received. He had received three other hats but the cowboy hat caught his attention. Melvin would again stand in front of the mirror and study the little cowboy he saw looking back at him. He would wave and smile at his new friend. The little boy in the full length hallway mirror became Melvin's daily companion. They would wear a different hat every day.

Melvin even found his old Easter bunny hat with one ear missing and wore it one day until the puppy showed his love for bunny ears. Melvin and his mirror friend watched as the puppy disappeared down the hallway. By the time Melvin had alerted his mother, the bunny hat was missing its other ear. Melvin watched with disappointment as his mother threw the hat in the trash can.

Melvin was no longer a bald headed little boy. His dad had already taken him to the barber shop which proved to be interesting as Melvin did not want his hat taken off. After some gentle coaxing, his hat was removed but he had to hold onto it. As soon as the last hair was cut, his little hat went back on his head. Melvin's love for hats never ceased. One day while his mom was shopping in a store, he saw a red hat with dog ears. He was not satisfied until it was on his head. He loved the hat and would spend many hours talking to his friend in the mirror who also wore a hat just like his. His puppy was older now and would sit by him while he visited with his friend but must of learned that Melvin's hats were not something to chew on. The puppy did eye Melvin nervously when Melvin wore the Mickey Mouse hat he had gotten for his second birthday.

When Melvin celebrated his third birthday, he received a football helmet which fit him perfectly. He loved the helmet and it was never taken off during the day until bath time. As soon as he was finished bathing, he put the helmet back on. He even tried to go to bed with his helmet on. His dad had a battle but finally convinced his son he would sleep much better with his Santa Claus hat on. His dog just smelled the helmet but never tried to chew on it. Instead of stealing Melvin's hats now, his dog just licked him a lot.

When Melvin was four years old he noticed his dad and grandpa did not have hair on their head. He asked his dad.

"Do you know you don't have any hair dad?"

His dad replied.

"Yes son, the wind blew it off of my head one day when it was blowing hard during a thunder storm."

Melvin then walked over and crawled up on his grandpa's lap. He looked at his grandpa's head as he asked him.

"Do you know you don't have hair on your head Grandpa?"

"Melvin, in my younger days when I was a cowboy, I would ride real fast and my cowboy hat would blow off in the wind. By the time I could stop my horse and ride back to pick up my hat, the wind had blown my hair out. My hair never grew back in. Be sure to always wear your hat outside. If your hair falls out, the hat will catch it."

Grandpa gave his grandson a wink and a hug. Melvin always remembered his dad's and grandpa's stories. He would wear his hat all the time so he would never be bald headed.

On Melvin's fifth birthday, his grandpa gave him a red hat with a character called Elmo on it. This became his favorite hat. He wanted to wear it to church but his mom told him.

"Melvin, you definitely are not going to wear that hat to church."

Melvin knew she meant business so he went to his bedroom and traded it for the hat his mom had bought special for this occasion. As soon as he got home, he quickly traded hats again and put Elmo back on his head where it belonged. One day Melvin's play was interrupted with a trip with his mother to go shopping for school supplies. It was time to him to start Kindergarten. He was excited because he would get to meet new friends and ride on the big yellow school bus. Two days before school officially started, Melvin's mother took him to school to meet his teacher. He liked her when he was introduced to her. She took him by his hand and showed him the desk where he would be sitting. It had his name on a card taped to the desk. Yes, he was going to like school. He did wear his Elmo hat that day and on the first day of school. When he got to school the first day he was shown where to put his backpack and his hat. He put his backpack in the cubicle assigned to him but not his hat. When the bell rang for the class to begin, the teacher looked out over her young students. Some were crying because they missed their mom already. Some did not want to sit at their desk. They wanted to explore their new surroundings. One student sat quietly at his desk as instructed by his mom and still wore his Elmo hat.

The teacher asked the ones roaming around to please sit down at their desk. Some of them did and some did not. She tried to calm the children who were crying. Some children did stop crying but they could not quit sniffling. She stopped by Melvin's desk and asked him to please take his hat off and put it with his backpack. Melvin refused and would not remove his hat. The teacher gave a sigh. She would give him time to adjust. Melvin wore his hat for the first two weeks of school to class, to lunch and to recess. He was never without it on his head. One day she asked him.

"Melvin, why do you wear your hat all the time?"

Melvin looked at her with a very serious look on his little face and answered.

"If I take my hat off I will be bald headed like my dad and grandpa. My grandpa told me it would catch my hair if it fell out and I could put it back on my head. It will keep the wind from blowing my hair away too. That is why; besides I like my hat."

The teacher gave Melvin a gentle smile; now she understood why he refused to take his hat off. She never mentioned it again until the first parent-teacher conference was scheduled. During the conference she told Melvin's mother what he had told her and why he refused to remove his hat. Melvin's dad was working and could not get off work to go to the conference. Melvin's mother promised to talk to Melvin but first she would talk to grandpa when she got home and to her husband when he got off work.

Grandpa was sitting on the front porch when she stopped to talk to him and pick up Melvin. Melvin had stayed with his Grandma and Grandpa while his mother went to see his teacher. When she told Grandpa about the conversation with the teacher, he grinned and got up to talk to his grandson. He found Melvin in the kitchen with Grandma eating cookies. He sat down and ate a cookie and then asked Melvin to come out on the porch and swing with him while they had a talk. Grandpa picked up two more cookies when Grandma was not looking and winked at Melvin. He walked to the front porch with Melvin following his footsteps.

They sat on the swing sharing the two cookies first then Grandpa said.

"Melvin, I need to talk to you about hats and getting baldheaded. What I told you is not true. I did not want to scare you about what really happened to my hair. The truth is I was riding my horse fast, but I was trying to get away from a war party of Indians. They Indians shot me with an arrow and I fell off of my horse. The Indians scalped me and left me for dead. Scalping means they take a knife or tomahawk and cut the skin off the top of your head with your hair. Indians don't do that any more. They only did that in the old days. My faithful old horse knelt down so I could crawl on its back after the war party left. My horse carried me to the nearest town where a doctor treated me. My hair was gone forever and to this very day is probably on an old Indian lance somewhere. Your dad became baldheaded when he got older because he made a wish on a star when he was your age to have hair just like me. His wish came true. You can take your hat off at school in the classroom and not worry about going bald. You should anyway, because young ladies are present and a gentleman should always take his hat off when inside a building and especially when ladies are present. Be sure to wear you hat outside though because the sun can give you skin cancer,"

The next day when Melvin came into the classroom, he put his backpack and hat in his cubicle. He walked over to the teacher's desk and told her what his Grandpa had told him. His teacher smiled and gave him a gentle pat on top of his head. His hair was soft and curly. She also watched with interest when they went to recess and he wore his hat. He did not want cancer, whatever that is. It must be bad or his Grandpa would not have warned him about wearing his hat outside.

The Kitchen Broom

WRITTEN BY
LLOYD WRIGHT

The Kitchen Broom

Granny was sitting at the kitchen table waiting for her great grandson Garrett. Gramps had been outside just piddling around. He looked at his watch as he went into the house to wait for his great grandson. As he walked in the door he said.

"Well Granny, it is about time for Garrett to get off the school bus."

They both looked forward to visiting with him and helping him with his homework after school. He rode on the bus to their house and stayed with them until his parents came home from work. Then Gramps saw what Granny was looking at. There in the center of the kitchen floor stood the kitchen broom. It was standing all by its self. Gramps looked at Granny and then the broom. Granny said.

"You know Gramps, this is the month of October. I have been told this is the month brooms can stand by themselves."

Gramps smiled and replied.

"Granny, you are absolutely right. Let's leave it standing there and see what Garrett has to say about the standing broom."

They watched out the kitchen window as the bus stopped at the end of the driveway and their great grandson hopped down the steps. He had his backpack slung over his shoulder as he sauntered toward the house. He always liked to look around and wave to his friends or anyone else who happened to go by. As soon as he opened the kitchen door and stepped in, he saw the standing broom. He immediately asked about the broom. Gramps smiled as he said.

"It is a witches broom"

Granny quickly replied.

"Garrett, during the month of October brooms can stand up. When I walked into the kitchen to wait for you, there it stood."

He took off his shoes by the door as he cautiously eyed the broom. Granny always made him take his shoes off by the door because he always had tons of sand in his shoes from the school playground. After he had taken off his shoes he circled around the broom and looked in the refrigerator for something to eat. After he had selected his snack, he crawled upon a chair by the table to eat it. Gramps watched him eat his snack. As soon as he had finished his snack and found something to drink, Gramps said.

"Garrett my boy, why don't you take that broom home with you? It kinda makes me nervous standing there. I know it has a spell cast on it."

Garrett quickly answered.

"Grandpa, I don't want that broom; you know my bedroom is dark."

Gramps did not pursue it anymore, he knew his grandson lived out in the country where the only yard light was the moon.

He did say.

"Witches do fly good in the country when the moon shines. They don't have to watch out for all the city buildings."

When Garrett finished his homework and his mother came to pick him up to take him home, she also saw the broom. Garrett left that evening without his grandma's kitchen broom.

The very next day Granny's broom did leave the kitchen. It left with Gramps when he went to school to visit two kindergarten classes. After Gramps had parked his truck, he took the bag out with the Halloween books he was going to read to the kindergarten students. He also took out Granny's broom. He kind of let the broom jerk around as he walked down the sidewalk. Individuals walking down the sidewalk eyed Gramps but never said a word. Some of the students he had read to when they were in kindergarten knew he was up to no good.

When Gramps walked into the classroom, a class full of smiling faces greeted him with a cheery, "Gramps."

Gramps stood the broom up on the floor and walked away from it. He eyed the broom as he sat down to read to them. He said.

"Watch that broom and let me know if it does anything strange. You know it is a witches broom and they can stand up during the month of October."

Gramps started to read about a nightmare in the attic when the computer in the room made a noise. Gramps stopped reading and asked the children.

"What made that noise?"

The class quickly replied.

"It was the broom."

Gramps moved his chair a little farther away from the broom and then continued reading. When he finished reading, "Something in the Attic," he read about, "Something in My Closet."

One boy in the class has slowly moved his chair closer to the broom. Curiosity was getting the best of him. Gramps watched him out of the corner of his eye as he worked his little chair closer to the broom. When he felt he was close enough he started to reach out to touch it. His little hand was stopped in midair when all his classmates yelled.

"Don't touch it; that is a witches broom!"

He quickly jerked his hand back. He looked at Gramps with his wide brown eyes and said.

"I don't think I will sleep good tonight!"

Gramps smiled as he said.

"I don't think there really is witches, I hope."

As Gramps was telling him about witches, he was eyeing Gramps sparse hair. When gramps had removed his hat when he entered the building, it made some of his sparse hair stand up. He ask.

"Why is your hair standing up?"

Gramps replied.

"It is the broom; I am afraid of it."

Gramps put his Halloween story book in his bag and stood up. He very cautiously approached the broom. When he grabbed it, it jerked around and tried to get away. All the class silently watched as Gramps departed the room. When he arrived at the next room the same scene was repeated. He left that class wondering about the standing broom that Gramps was afraid of.

As Gramps drove home, he thought about the standing broom. He had ridden a kitchen broom as his horse hunting outlaws when he was the same age as the kindergarten students. If Granny wasn't watching maybe he would ride this broom around the yard behind his truck where no one would see him. He didn't even know if he could ride a stick horse. He had two artificial knees and an artificial hip. When he visited the Grand Canyon a few years ago, he had a hard time getting upon the back of a mule.

When Gramps pulled into the carport, he did not see anyone in sight. He got out of the truck and opened the back door. He got out Granny's kitchen broom and as he leaned against the truck, he straddled the broom. Just as he settled down in the saddle he heard a voice say.

"Hey, aren't you a little old to be riding a broom."

Gramps looked up with embarrassment. It was a neighbor out for a walk. Gramps waved as the stick broom bucked. When the neighbor was out of sight, Gramps tried to fly the broom just like a witch would. Using his imagination just like he did years ago when he hunted outlaws with his stick horse, Gramps flew high in the air.

Santa And The Grand Canyon

Written By
Lloyd Wright

Santa And The Grand Canyon

Santa was sitting on a bale of hay in the reindeer barn. He had just finished his breakfast and must now get busy checking the reindeer harness. Christmas was fast approaching. The elves were busy in the workshops filling the Christmas list Santa must deliver Christmas Eve. As Santa was checking the harness and rubbing oil into the leather to keep it from getting stiff and hard, he thought about Gramps. Gramps, along with children he reads to, had visited him for the last few years. This year he had sent Wayne the Christmas Tree Elf to see Gramps and invite three classes whose teachers had never been to the North Pole. A teacher by the name of Mrs. Debbie Finch and her class had visited the last several years. This year he has a very special trip planned for Mrs. Finch and her class. Gramps had told Mrs. Finch several time she must see the Grand Canyon. Santa had visited it every year but it was always dark. Just one time he would like to see it as the morning sun paints it with color.

Santa got up from the bale of hay and went looking for Rufus, the oldest elf. Rufus is the foreman who takes care of the reindeer and the sleighs. Santa has several sleighs. He has a cargo sleigh he uses to haul supplies for the North Pole. He has a carriage sleigh, which is special built to haul passengers in. It is all enclosed and heated. Then he has the Christmas sleigh. It is painted red and has twinkling Christmas lights and bells mounted on it. This is the sleigh he uses to deliver presents on Christmas Eve. It is pulled by his special team of reindeer. These reindeer are fast and can pull for a long distance. His cargo reindeer team are big and slow but can pull several tons of supplies through the air on the cargo sleigh.

Santa found Rufus in the sleigh shed polishing the runners on Santa's Christmas sleigh. The runners must be kept especially clean so they will glide through the snow with no resistance. With very little distance to gather enough speed to fly off of house tops it required the sleigh and runners be in top condition. When Santa found Rufus he asked him to check out the carriage sleigh. He has a special trip planned for it shortly. After talking to Rufus, Santa needed to find Miss Matilda. She is the principal for the North Pole school system for elves. He has a special mission to send her on. He wanted her to visit Mrs. Finch's classroom and make arrangements for the trip.

Mrs. Finch was reading to her kindergarten when she heard a slight knock on her classroom door. She walked over to see who was knocking. When she opened the door, there stood a pleasant little elf lady. She did not need to introduce herself; the two ladies had met at the North Pole. Mrs. Finch knew she was the Principal for the North Pole School System. She had visited the school during her visits to the North Pole with Little Toot and Gramps. Mrs. Finch invited Miss Matilda into the classroom. The children were very inquisitive about the visitor. Mrs. Finch introduced Matilda to the students as follows to Miss Matilda.

"Miss Matilda, I would like for you to meet Jesse, Ryan, Parker, Zayda, Lindsay, Larry, Lauren, Robnyzah, David, Isidro, Sophie, Aidan, Devin, Jamar, Emily, Azayla, and Michael."

Miss Matilda took the time to shake each students hand. She then turned to Mrs. Finch and said.

"Mrs. Finch, I know you are busy so I will get right to the point why I am here. Santa wants to take you and your students to visit the Grand Canyon. He has always wanted to see it in the daylight and he knows Gramps has encouraged you to visit it. As the sun is rising over the horizon the day after school lets out for Christmas vacation, he would like to load all of you in his carriage sleigh for the trip. He said to tell you the deer can fly faster than the speed of light. The children will only be gone for one day. I will be back for your answer in one week."

Miss Matilda smiled and waved to the students as she disappeared out of the classroom door. Mrs. Finch hadn't even had a chance to tell her good-by. She hurried over to the door and looked out into the hallway. Miss Matilda was no where in sight. The students were very bubbly with excitement. Mrs. Finch sent a note home with each of her students asking for the parent's permission for their child to make the trip with their classmates.

Miss Matilda returned to Mrs. Finch's classroom a week later as promised. She found Mrs. Finch busy with paper work as Gramps read a story to the students. She was glad Gramps was there because Santa wanted him to accompany the class to the Grand Canyon. He had told Santa he had visited the Grand Canyon several times. It was one of his favorite National Parks to visit. Gramps has a Gold Card to visit national parks. Mrs. Finch got up from her desk and walked over and gave Miss Matilda a hug. She then told her all of her students had received permission from their parents to take the trip. Miss Matilda could see how excited the children were over the thought of taking a trip with Santa Claus. It was arranged for Santa to land across the street from Mrs. Finch's home at the time planned on the old railroad right-a-away.

The sun was just peeking over the horizon the first day of Christmas vacation as Santa appeared out of nowhere and landed. The students were with their parents sitting in their cars keeping warm as they had waited. Santa jumped out of the sleigh as soon as it has come to a stop and beckoned to Mrs. Finch and the children. The children lined up to get in the sleigh. Mrs. Finch called out the children's name; Jesse, Ryan, Parker, Zayda, Lindsay, Larry, Lauren, Robnyzah, David, Isidro, Sophie, Aidan, Devin, Jamar, Emily. Azayla, and Michael. As their names were called, Santa helped each student into the sleigh. He asked Gramps to ride in the front with him so they could visit during the flight. Mrs. Finch followed the children into the carriage sleigh with Santa's helping hand. The children were all snuggled in warm blankets by the time Santa picked up the reins and said.

"Now Dasher! Now Dancer! Now Prancer and Vixen! On Comet! On Cupid! On Donner and Blitzen! Dash away! Dash away! Dash away all!"

The parents watched as the reindeer and sleigh climbed into the sky and turned to the west. They gained speed rapidly and was soon out of sight. The children were warm and cozy in the carriage sleigh. They watched the land below go by swiftly as they flew over the state of Arkansas and Oklahoma. Soon they could see the snow covered Rocky Mountains. Mrs. Finch was using this opportunity to teach her class geography. Most of the students had never saw mountains. Santa flew lower so they could have a greater view. They followed the Colorado River as it flowed to the southwest. Mrs. Finch told her class about the river and its importance. It furnished water to irrigate farm land, drinking water, and electricity to the southwestern United States.

Santa interrupted the flight long enough to land at the Petrified Forest. Mrs. Finch explained to her class how forests were petrified. The children wanted to get out and collect some petrified wood. Mrs. Finch explained if everyone took some wood from there it would ruin the Petrified Forest for others to see. The stay was short but informative. Santa softly spoke to his reindeer and they were soon airborne. He flew low over the Painted Desert as they approached the Grand Canyon. With the early morning sun shining it made a spectacular view.

Santa had been right about his reindeer's speed. They had kept up with the sun and were landing at the Grand Canyon as the early morning sun reflected off the walls of the canyon. Before they landed, Santa flew down through the canyon to give his passengers a view they will never forget. Santa and Gramps enjoyed the beauty they saw from their vantage point. Mrs. Finch was no longer talking to her students. She was in awe of what she was seeing. Gramps had been right, the people who do not visit the Grand Canyon during their lifetime are missing an indescribable sight. The reindeer flew on following the Colorado River until they were over Hoover Dam. It was such a massive structure to have been built by man. It was the lifeline to so many people. It was putting the great Colorado River to work.

Santa turned his reindeer back to the east and were soon landing on the south rim of the Grand Canyon. Gramps and Santa helped Mrs. Finch watch the children. None of them could believe what their eyes were seeing. The watched the colors change as they moved across the canyon walls. The Colorado River could be seen as a thin line one mile below them in the bottom of the canyon. Who could believe this great canyon had been carved over the years by its rushing water. The children were not the only ones looking in awe. There were people from many other nations there viewing this grandeur.

By this time everyone's stomachs were growling. Gramps told them about the restaurant he had eaten in before located right on the rim. When Santa was told they served biscuits and gravy he knew that was the place to go. They were all soon seated after they had washed their hands. The waitress gave them special attention. No one questioned about Santa since it was the Christmas Season. Santa did have a double order of biscuits and gravy. The children all found their favorite breakfast on the menu. Gramps ate scrambled eggs, ham, hash browns and toast. Mrs. Finch ordered pancakes with fruit and whip cream on top.

After they had finished their breakfast, Gramps suggested they visit the mule corral and barn. The mules were used to carry tourist down into the canyon. He happened to like mules very much. When they arrived at the corral, the mules to be used for the journey into the canyon that day had been saddled and already left. There still were plenty of mules for the class to see. They did not make the mules work without a day to rest. When they went into the mule barn, the foreman recognized Gramps. Gramps introduced him to Mrs. Finch, the children, and Santa. Since the mules to be used that day had been fed and on there way into the canyon, the foreman said they had time to give the children a ride on some of the remaining mules if they would like a ride. All of the boys and four of the girls wanted a ride. Of course, Santa and Gramps got there turn also. After much persuasion, Mrs. Finch even rode a mule. When the rides were over, everyone thanked the mule barn foreman.

After a stop to drink a refreshment, it was decided to ride the Grand Canyon tour bus. From the visitor center they rode west to view Hopi Point. Next they visited Mohave Point and Prima Point. They stopped at Hermits Rest before their return to the visitor center. The class then boarded Santa's carriage. Santa followed Gramps directions and they visited Yaki Point. The next stop was at Grandview Point, which was appropriately named. Everyone walked out to the point and had a grand view of the great canyon. As they looked out over the canyon, Mrs. Finch was overwhelmed by the changing colors. She walked over to Santa and gave him a great big hug. As she hugged him, she thanked him for the great Christmas present he had so generously given to her class and herself. They watched as birds with their wings spread sailing around the canyon walls down below. The next stop was Moran Point. Each point they visited had a different view. The last Point to visit was Desert View. Again they stretched their legs as they enjoyed the view stretching out in front of them. The last stop before returning to eat a snack was Tusayan Ruin and Museum.

It was time to return to the restaurant and have something to eat before they returned home. The time had passed so quickly. No one was ready to leave the Grand Canyon. Santa and Gramps did not have a snack; they had a full course meal. The children enjoyed a sandwich with French Fries. Mrs. Finch ordered soup and a sandwich, which she enjoyed. The waitress served all cake and ice cream which nobody turned down. After everyone's hunger had been satisfied, it was time to get into the carriage sleigh. After the children were all accounted for and tucked in, Santa and Gramps crawled up on the sleigh. As surprised tourists watched, Santa picked up the reins and said.

Now Dasher! Now Dancer! Now Prancer and Vixen! On Comet! On Cupid! On Dancer and Blitzen! To the top of the top of the visitor center! To the top of the mule barn! Now Dash away! Dash away! Dash away all.

The class along with Mrs. Finch watched with sadness as the Great Grand Canyon disappeared behind them.

Old Man Halters

Written By
Lloyd Wright

Old Man Halters

Little Jimmy woke up to the smell of a hot breakfast cooking on the kitchen stove. His mother always insures he eats a hot breakfast before going to school for the day. Jimmy is in Kindergarten now and has to get up in time to eat his breakfast and walk to school. He lives six blocks from school and enjoys walking with his friend to school. After Jimmy washed his hands and face, and brushed his teeth, he bounced down the stairs with his backpack being dragged along behind. As he bounced down the stairs he sang a Christmas Carol he had been practicing at school for the Christmas Program. Jimmy crawled up to the kitchen table and when all were seated he bowed his head while his dad said thanks.

He was in a hurry today to meet his friend. They had seen a wooden rooster sitting on a front gate, and as the wind blew, it pecked on some seed glued on the gate post. Jimmy and his friend wanted to take a closer look at it. While they were eating, his mother said to his dad.

"Jim, the kitchen faucet has been leaking for the past month. The commode also runs most of the time. This morning I noticed one of the kitchen cabinets is in need of repair and two light bulbs are burnt out in the living room. I know you are busy at work but maybe next Saturday you could find enough time to at least look at them."

Jim looked at his wife as he replied.

"I will call Old Man Halters when I get to work. He is retired and a Jack-Of-All Trades. I know he can fix everything you just mentioned and can also use the money to supplement his retired pay."

Jimmy listened with interest and then he asked his dad.

"Who is Old Man Halters and what does a Jack-Of-All Trades mean?"

Little Jimmy's dad gave a startled look at his son and then replied.

"Jimmy, I should not have called Mr. Halters, "Old Man Halters," I was wrong. I should show more respect toward him. Just remember, when you talk to adults, call them Mr. or Mrs.

Now the answer to your other question, what is a Jack-Of-All Trades? A Jack-Of-All Trades has the knowledge and ability to repair everything. The work he had done throughout his lifetime has given him this knowledge."

Jimmy made his breakfast disappear in record time. His mother said.

"Jimmy, why are you in such a hurry? You ate your breakfast so fast I don't think you even tasted it."

Jimmy replied.

"My friend and I have something we want to look at on our way to school."

After Jimmy met his friend, they ran to get where the wooden rooster was sitting on a gate pecking as the wind blew. They were so interested in the rooster, they did not hear or see the owner and maker of the rooster, walk over to where they were standing. He said.

"Good morning boys, it is sure a fine day to be looking at roosters."

They looked up and saw an old man with white hair and a long white beard smiling at them and with a twinkle in his eye. The boys thought for a minute they were seeing Santa Claus. The old fellow told the boys since he had nothing better to do he made the wooden rooster in his work shop. Jimmy said.

"I sure like your rooster; I wish I knew how to make things like that."

The old man smiled and replied.

"Maybe someday you will if you want to learn how to bad enough."

Jimmy liked the old man. He picked up his backpack where he had set it down and said.

"Thank you for letting us look at your rooster. We have to go to school now, good-by."

The boys ran the rest of the way to school. Jimmy thought about the man who looked like Santa Claus all during the school day. He told his teacher about the man and the wooden rooster that pecks. When the school day was over, Jimmy and his friend ran to look at the rooster. They did not see the nice old man. They did not look at the rooster long though; they both knew their mothers would be waiting for them.

When Jimmy arrived home he yelled.

"Mom, I am home, where are you?"

His mom answered.

"I am in the kitchen Jimmy."

When Jimmy walked into the kitchen he saw the old man who looked like Santa Claus, working on the kitchen faucets. Jimmy walked over and after watching him for a couple minutes said.

"Hi, my friend and I stopped to watch your rooster eat on our way home from school."

Jimmy's mom said.

"Jimmy this is Mr. Halters, now don't bother him while he is working."

Mr. Halters stopped and while he shook Jimmy's hand, he said.

"I am pleased to meet you Jimmy. You and your friend are welcome to look at the rooster any time you want."

As Jimmy was shaking Mr. Halters hand, he said.

"This morning when my friend and I saw you, we thought you were Santa Claus. Mom this is the nice man with a wooden rooster on his gate."

Mr. Halters chuckled as he said.

"Most folks just call me Old Man Halters."

Jimmy replied.

"My dad called you Old Man Halters this morning and then he told me your name is Mr. Halters and to always call adults Mrs. or Mr."

Jimmy's mom turned red from embarrassment and started to apologize but Mr. Halters chuckled as he said.

"No need to apologize; I think Jimmy is a fine young man and meant no harm."

Jimmy looked at his mom and said.

"I am sorry mom."

Jimmy watched as Mr. Halters turned the water on and checked for leaks. When he was sure the faucet was fixed, he picked up his tools and walked over to repair the kitchen cabinet. He said.

"Jimmy, would you like to help me fix this cabinet? It sure would be a lot of help if you would hand me my tools when I need them."

When Mr. Halters was finished repairing all that needed repaired, Jimmy helped him put the tools in his tool box.

Mr. Halters shook Jimmy's hand and thanked him for his help. When he was ready to leave he said to Jimmy and his mom.

"I have a work shop in my back yard where I make different things from scrap wood. Jimmy and his dad are welcome to visit me anytime. I may need Jimmy's help making Christmas gifts for children in need. The things I make during the year I take to the people collecting Christmas gifts for foster children. A friend gives me all the scrap wood he has left from building houses. I appreciate his generosity and it give me something to do."

The next Saturday Jimmy was playing a game in the living room. His dad sat in his recliner watching television. Jimmy thought about Mr. Halters and his work shop. Jimmy walked over and leaned against his dad's chair and said.

"Dad, when Mr. Halters was here he told mom and me that we were welcome to visit him anytime. Is it anytime now?"

Jimmy's mother heard the conversation and said.

"Jim, I think anytime is now. You need to spend time with your son plus I need to clean in here and you two are in the way."

Jim slowly got up from his recliner and said.

"Jimmy get your hat and coat on and we will get out of here and go visit Mr. Halters faster than a herd of turtles."

Jimmy could see his breath as they walked through the snow to Mr. Halters' house. They saw smoke drifting up from the chimney on the work shop. They could hear an electric sander running as they knocked on the shed door by pulling a string attached to a red headed woodpecker mounted on the door as a door knocker. Jimmy was still admiring the door knocker when Mr. Halters opened the door. He had a big smile on his face and welcomed them with a hardy handshake. He had a small wood stove in the center of his shop keeping it toasty warm. He shut his radio off which was playing Christmas music so he could visit with his company. He liked to listen to music as he worked.

He showed them around his shop and showed them the toys he had lying up on the rafters and in every corner. Jimmy could see Mrs. Halters had been busy making gifts for Christmas. He said.

"Jimmy, crawl up on that stool and I'll give you a board to pound nails in."

Jimmy had never used a hammer or driven a nail. Mr. Halters showed him how and then handed him the hammer and a couple of nails. Jimmy held the nail with one hand and lifted the hammer with the other. When he went to hit the nail he hit his thumb. He jumped down off of the stool and did a little dance as he held his thumb. Mr. Halters smiled as he said.

"Jimmy, you are supposed to hit the other nail, not your thumb nail."

Jimmy's dad laughed as he watched his son do an Indian dance holding his thumb. He watched as Jimmy finally crawled back up on the stool and tried driving the nail again. This time he hit the nail instead of his thumb. Jim and Mr. Halters visited as Jimmy drove nails. He was a quick learner and only did one more dance while driving nails. Mr. Halters had Jimmy hand him some fire wood to put in the stove when it starting to cool down. Jimmy's dad then said.

Mr. Halters, you did a fine job fixing the things in my house. It pleased my wife, which pleased me. We have wasted enough of your time but sure have enjoyed our visit. Mr. Halters shook Jimmy's hand as he said.

Jim, let your boy come back anytime. I sure could use his help since he knows how to drive the right nail. I do get kind of lonely and would enjoy his company. You are welcome anytime too. As Jimmy and his dad left the yard they could hear Mrs. Halters singing a Christmas carol.

Jimmy showed his dad the pecking rooster before they walked home. Mr. Halters started working on a wooden pecking rooster to give to Jimmy for Christmas. He would paint it red just like his. He may just make a red headed woodpecker for Jimmy to put on his bedroom door. Yes sir, he sure liked that boy. As Jimmy skipped along beside his dad going home he said.

"Dad, you know Mr. Halters does not live at the North Pole but I still think he is Santa Claus.

Jimmy's dad patted him on the shoulder as he replied.

"I think you may just be right son."

A Special Turkey

Written By
Lloyd Wright

A Special Turkey

The month of November had arrived along with special school homework concerning a turkey. Garrett looked at the papers with a turkey drawn on it and the instruction on what he was to do with it. He read with interest that he was supposed to cut out the turkey and put it on poster board. Then he was supposed to use his own imagination and decorate it. He could color it or put other things on it. He was also supposed to write a story about how his family celebrates Thanksgiving. All this homework was required to be completed and returned to his school teacher, Mrs. Holmes by November 17th.

Garrett knew all about turkeys. He had hunted wild turkey with his Dad and his Grandpa. He knew how to use a turkey call and put out decoys. Before he was three years old he could make a sound like a turkey call with his mouth and voice. He was always asked to make that sound when the relatives gathered for holidays. He knew to wear camouflage clothing and how to watch the woods for movement. He knew what signs to look for in the woods. He had watched his dad and Grandpa dress a turkey and cook it. Maybe he could put real feathers on his paper turkey.

His great grandpa had told him stories about when he was in high school and worked part time on a commercial tame turkeys farm. He had said.

"Garrett, you know tame turkeys are not very smart at all. When it rains they will look up to see where it is coming from and the rain will run up their nostrils and drown them. The fence to keep them penned in has to be built zigzag. Turkeys will stampede just like cattle on the open range when it storms. A zigzag fence can be knocked down by the stampeding turkeys and they will not smother or crush themselves. A fence with ninety degree corners will kill a stampeding flock as they get piled up in the corners and a straight fence is harder to knock down. Whenever a storm was forecast we had to herd the turkeys into their houses."

Garrett knew all about turkeys, but decorating a paper turkey on a poster was not the same as hunting a turkey. Hunting was a lot more fun. Garrett put his homework in his backpack to take home. He would ask his mom or dad to help him. He would also show the paper turkey to his great grandma and great grandpa.

Garrett carried his paper turkey home on the school bus in his backpack. He half carried the backpack and half drug it into his great grandma's house. As he was getting his snack to eat, Grandma looked in his backpack to see if he had any homework. Garrett showed her the turkey and showed her the instructions. She did give him some ideas. Gramps just eyed the turkey and said.

"Garrett, if you make it look good enough maybe Granny will cook it for Thanksgiving."

Garrett put it back in his backpack for safe keeping. He would show it to his mom when she came to take him home.

Garrett's mom looked in his backpack after she had fed her family their evening meal. She looked at his assignment concerning the paper turkey. She planned on buying the necessary poster board the next day. Garrett had already told his dad about the turkey and let him know that some real turkey feathers would make his turkey look real. Garrett did color the turkey's head and feet. He got his scissors and as his mom watched, he very carefully started to cut the paper turkey out. He was concentrating so hard on the work, it made his tongue stick out of his mouth. His mother said.

"Garrett, if you aren't careful you will cut your tongue off."

Garrett's mom did buy poster board for the turkey. Garrett pasted it on the board. He took a sack and went out to the back yard to look for something to put on the poster board by the turkey's feet. He pulled some dried grass, picked up some twigs, and little rocks. He went into the house and glued them on the board. The next day after school, he picked up some brightly colored leaves and several acorns from his great grandpa's yard. When he got home he glued the acorns among the dead oak leaves onto the board toward the bottom where his turkey could walk on the leaves and find the acorns. He placed some of the twigs he had gathered on the side like they were part of the woods. He glued the brightly colored leaves like they were in the air falling toward the ground. He did get a variety of feathers from his dad to glue on the turkey. He had colored the turkey and glued the feathers so they blended in. He sure liked his turkey; it looked good enough to put in the woods for a turkey decoy. He would not show it to Gramps because he would want Granny to stuff and roast it for Thanksgiving.

As he looked as his paper turkey, he thought about the story he had to write. His dad wanted fish for Thanksgiving and remembered his dad telling his mom.

"Beth, this year I will deep fry fish for Thanksgiving."

His mom had told his dad.

"Mike, if you want fish for Thanksgiving, they better had gobbled and grew feathers during their lifetime! We are going to have turkey!"

Garrett knew then, along with his dad, they would be eating turkey.

Garrett starting writing his story.

Every year Mom and Dad invite their family for Thanksgiving. They all bring some food to help Mom feed that many people. Mom buys a big frozen turkey and puts it in the refrigerator a few days before so it will thaw. The day before Thanksgiving she has my dad and me clean and wash the turkey inside and out. Mom gives my dad a big towel to wrap the turkey in and he puts it back in the refrigerator. While we are doing that, mom is busy baking pies.

On Thanksgiving morning Mom has my dad get the turkey out of the refrigerator and put it in a big roasting pan with a lid. My dad helps Mom stuff the turkey with dressing. When it is stuffed, Mom puts some water in the pan and some salt and pepper on the turkey. Dad puts it in the oven and soon the kitchen smells like Thanksgiving.

Mom cooks potatoes, vegetables and boils some hard eggs. She makes a lot of other stuff too.

The company arrives and all bring food. Grandma and my aunts help Mom cook and set the table. She makes Dad check the turkey a lot and squirt stuff from the pan on it. My aunts tells all of us kids to get out of the way and go play. They tell the men to go get lost. My mom tells my dad.

"Don't you try to get lost. I need you to watch the turkey and take it out when it is done."

It seems like I will starve to death before Thanksgiving dinner is ready. Finally we get to sit down at the table and eat after we have all washed our hands. After dinner, my mom and aunts do the dishes. My dad, Uncles and Grandpa watch football and sleep.

After all the company has gone home, my mom says.

"It took a week to get everything ready and cook it. They all come and sit down and make it disappear in a few minutes!"

Yuk, we always eat leftovers for a week so I know they don't eat it all.

That is how we spend Thanksgiving.

Garrett did show Gramps his turkey when it was done. Gramps really liked it and did not have Granny roast it for Thanksgiving. He took the fine looking turkey and his Thanksgiving story to school before November 17th. He did hope his teacher liked it as much as he did and would takes good care of his turkey.

Gifts To Give

Written By
Lloyd Wright

Gifts To Give

As little Herald Jr. got off the school bus, he was in deep thought. His teacher had asked her kindergarten class to bring a Christmas gift to school to give to someone in need instead of drawing names for each other. His mom and dad were in need. He didn't have any money and he had heard his mom and dad talking one night. They thought he was in bed sound asleep. His dad had been laid off from his job and his mom was cleaning homes for other people to help pay the bills. His dad did find part time work, sometimes. He helped the man selling Christmas trees on week ends when he needed help. It worried Herald; he wanted to take a gift to school, but what?

When he walked into the house, his mom was in the kitchen starting to make soup for supper. His dad was in the back yard raking leaves. After he changed into his play clothes, he ran out the back door to help his dad. They raked the leaves into a pile and then set them on fire. They sat down on the back porch steps with the garden hose and watched the leaves burn. As they sat there, Herald Jr. said.

"Dad, my teacher wants me to bring a gift for someone in need. I don't have any money to buy a gift."

Herald Sr. hugged his son as he said.

"Son, it hurts me to tell you this, but I don't have any money to spare. We have bills to pay and we just may not have any money left over for Christmas, and I refuse to ask your grandpa for help."

Little Herald was doing his school homework after supper when the phone rang. His mother answered the phone and he heard her say.

"Hello. Just a minute Grandpa; you can ask him yourself. I know he would be happy to help you next Saturday."

Little Herald's mother handed him the telephone. After he had answered the telephone, he heard Grandpa say.

"Herald, I need help cutting firewood for the fireplace next Saturday. If you will help me, I will bring old Lucille, the truck, and pick you up. You can eat breakfast with Grandma and me. You will have to get up early so we will have time to work up an appetite for lunch. Grandma plans to have us catch a rooster so she can fry it for lunch. She has already made an apple pie from the apples we picked from the apple tree in the yard the last time you were here."

Herald was all smiles as he told Grandpa.

"Yes, I will help you Grandpa. I will get up early and be ready when you and Lucille get here. I hope I get to eat a fried chicken leg."

Little Herald was looking out the kitchen window when Grandpa turned Lucille into the driveway. He already had his hat and coat on. As he ran to go out the kitchen door he said.

"Good-by Mom, Grandpa is here."

Out the door he ran to greet Grandpa. Grandpa had the door open for him to hop in. Little Herald didn't even slow down when he jumped in the truck and gave Grandpa a hug. After he had closed Lucille's door and buckled his seat belt, Grandpa backed out of the driveway as he said.

"Good morning Herald, hang on to your hat, we are off faster than a speeding turtle."

After they were on the country road leading to Grandpa's house, Grandpa let Little Herald sit on his lap and drive old Lucille. This was his favorite time when he went to Grandma and Grandpa's house except maybe eating Grandma's cooking. When they turned into the farm driveway, there was old Ned to greet them. Ned is Grandpa's "do all" dog. He is a cattle dog, watch dog, hunting dog, Grandson licker and a good listener, at least that is what Grandpa says. Grandpa must be right because when Little Herald jumped out of the truck, Ned greeted him with a wet dog lick.

Ned followed Grandpa and Herald to the house. They could smell the aroma of breakfast cooking as they walked up on the back porch. Ned followed his sniffing nose right to the back door, but he knew he could not go in. He watched as Grandpa and Herald disappeared in the back door. He laid down by the door and waited; he knew he would be getting his breakfast soon.

Grandma swooped Little Herald up in her arms at the door with a great big hug. She then proceeded to kiss his cheeks until they were rosy. After her greeting, it was time to wash their hands and eat breakfast. He had his choice of cold cereal, fried eggs, bacon, toast, biscuits and gravy. Grandpa skipped the cold cereal and sampled all of the rest. He decided to eat fried eggs, bacon, and toast with home made jelly. Grandpa had advised him to eat a hot meal because he was going to work his britches off.

After they had eaten breakfast, they put on their coats and hat. As they were heading toward the back door Grandma said.

"Boys, don't forget to catch a young rooster and pick it if you want fried chicken for dinner."

Before they started working on the woodpile, they did catch a young rooster and got it ready for Grandma. When that job was done, they went to the woodpile. Grandpa split the wood with an axe and Little Herald carried it to the woodpile and stacked it. After they had worked for an hour, Grandpa said.

"Herald, I need a rest. You are working me too hard. Sit over here on this log with me and tell me what is on your mind. I can tell something is bothering you. You know there is a never a problem that can't be fixed."

Little Herald crawled upon the log and sat next to his grandpa. His eyes were misty as he looked up at Grandpa's. He said.

"Grandpa, my teacher at school wants everyone in my class to bring a Christmas gift to school to give to somebody in need instead of drawing names for each other. I don't have any money and my mom and dad are in need. I told dad I didn't have any money to buy a gift. He told me we may not even have a Christmas since he is out of work and Mom cleans houses to buy food. What can I do Grandpa?"

Grandpa gave his grandson a hug as he said.

"Herald, you sure have been carrying a worrisome load on your shoulders for someone your age. First off, you will have Christmas at your house! Santa Claus never misses a home. Now you have a lot of gifts to give. When you were born you gave a gift money can not buy. You made Grandma and me grandparents. You have given us so much happiness. When you gave Grandma a hug and kiss this morning, you gave her joy. You helped me catch the rooster for dinner and been helping me cut wood for the fireplace. Those are all gift that didn't cost you a nickel. You help your neighbor lady when you run errands for her. You give a gift to your mom and dad when you help them. You may not realize it but you give them a gift when you are good. You can give your teacher a huge gift by offering to help her. You can help her by being quiet and listen in the classroom instead of making her write your name on the blackboard. You do not need money to give a gift. You have all kinds of gifts to give. I will call your school and ask if we can take your class on a hayride. I know your class has been practicing for your Christmas program. Maybe your class can sing those Christmas carols as we visit the needy. You know everybody is in need to hear children sing, even Grandma and me. I think it is time we get back to work so we can work up an appetite and give Grandma a gift by eating all of her fried chicken and mashed potatoes. I think she baked a cake if Ned and my smellers are working right. I know she has an apple pie."

When Grandma yelled.

"Dinner is ready, come on in and wash your hands before you sit down at my table!"

Grandpa and Little Herald walked hand in hand to the house with Ned leading the way. Herald helped his Grandma by eating two fried chicken legs and a big piece of cake and a piece of pie. Grandpa winked at Herald as he took a second piece of cake and said.

"I am giving Grandma a gift by helping this cake disappear."

Little Herald and Grandpa worked hard chopping wood and stacking it until Grandma stepped out on the back porch and said.

"Would you fellas like some hot chocolate and fresh oatmeal cookies for a snack? There is some cake and apple pie that needs eaten also"

Grandpa said.

"We will be right in as soon as I put the ax in the shed. We were just finishing up. Our Grandson has put in a hard days work."

Herald hugged his grandma as she swooped him off of his feet when he came in the back door. She hugged him and made his cheeks rosy again. He looked at Grandpa and saw him wink and smile. He knew what Grandpa was telling him. After they finished their snack, Herald hugged Grandma good-by and gave her a kiss. He said.

"I Love you Grandma."

Grandma walked out to old Lucille with him and opened the door for him. Grandpa and Lucille were all ready to take him home after a hard days work. Grandma waved as they drove out of the driveway. Grandpa said.

"Hang on to your hat, we are off faster than a speeding turtle."

After Herald had his bath and was ready for bed, he took his school tablet and sat at the kitchen table. He asked his mom if she would help him make a Christmas card for his teacher. He drew a picture of Santa Claus and wrote Merry Christmas. He also wrote, I love my teacher.

Monday morning after the everyone was in their seats, Herald held up his hand and said.

"I have something important to give to you."

The teacher said.

"What do you have Herald that is so important?"

Herald got up out of his seat and walked up to the teachers desk. He gave her a hug and handed her an envelope. He then said.

"You told us to bring a gift to school for someone in need. My grandpa said everybody needs a hug. He also told me I can give you a gift by being quiet and listening to you so you don't have to write my name on the blackboard. I promise to be as quiet as I can. My Grandpa wants me to help him put straw on his hayrack so he can take all of us on a hayride to sing Christmas Carols to everybody in need. He said, everybody needs to hear children sing, even him and Grandma. He told me to tell you that is my gift. Merry Christmas."

Herald started to turn around and walk back to his desk when his teacher said.

"Herald come here; you need a hug for listening to your Grandpa. You have given me a Christmas gift I will never forget."

The Doll In The Window

WRITTEN BY
LLOYD WRIGHT

The Doll In The Window

Mr. Wilson's Christmas shipment of toys had just arrived. After all these years, he knew what the children would want under the Christmas Tree. When he opened one of the boxes of dolls, one doll immediately attracted his attention. She reminded him of a little Angel. He decided right there and then to put her in the front window for display. He knew she would sell right away even though she sold for more money than any of the other dolls in the shipment. He carried the doll in her pretty Christmas decorated box to the front of the store by the large display window. As he was placing her in front of the window, a little girl stood like she was in a trance as she watched him. He recognized her as the little girl who sang with her mother on street corners for donations. He knew somehow he must see that this little girl received this doll. He put a sign on the doll, which read, For Display Only.

Little Jeannie was so interested looking at the doll in the Toy Store window, that she did not notice the cold through her worn thin jacket or hear her mother call her. She did not know her mother was standing beside her until her mother took her by the hand and said.

"Jeannie, you are wasting your time looking at that doll in the window. You know we can not afford anything like that."

Mr. Wilson had seen the lady who plays the guitar and sings with her daughter outside of his store. He hurried over and stepped outside. He said to her.

"I have heard you and your daughter sing Christmas carols. I would like to hire you and your daughter to sing in front of my store for five days during the week before Christmas, it would sure help my business. I will pay you and also give the doll in the window to your daughter for your service."

The hours they would sing and the pay was agreed upon. Little

Jeannie's mother was glad to have the work. She had been worried about buying gifts for Christmas and putting food on the table. She is a single mom and if Grandpa Fred hadn't insisted they come and live with him she did not know what she would have done.

Jeannie is in kindergarten and after the Christmas program tomorrow she would be on Christmas vacation. She knew Grandpa Fred would come and watch her sing at school. He always called her his little Angel. When she wasn't in school or singing on street corners with her mom, she was with him. Grandma had gone away to a special place right after little Jeannie was born. Grandpa had told her many times.

"Jeannie you may not be Grandma but you are a Blessing to me."

Grandpa Fred needed Jeannie and her mom, and they needed him.

The next day, Jeannie's mom had to work and Grandpa Fred attended the Kindergarten Christmas program. Jeannie had been chosen to be dressed like an angel and sing the carol, "Do You See What I See," as she held up a star on a stick. Yes sir, she was his angel and he was so proud of her.

After the Christmas program was over, the children were released from school for Christmas vacation. Just as they were leaving the school, Jeannie asked.

"Grandpa, can we stop at the toy store so I can look at the doll in the window. Mr. Wilson is giving her to me for singing with mom in front of his store."

His daughter had already told him about the part time job. Little Jeannie had told him about the doll in the window a hundred times. She sure was excited and could hardly wait until she had earned it singing Christmas carols.

Grandpa Fred looked at his granddaughter and said.

"We are on our way to see your, soon to be, playmate."

They parked in a spot close to the store and Jeannie went to look at the doll with Grandpa Fred. As her Grandpa looked at the doll in the window that was marked, For Display Only, he thought how the little doll reminded him of his little Jeannie. He wished he had enough money to buy it for her now, but he had too many bills to pay. His wife had been sick for a long time before she went away and the medical bills piled up faster then he could pay them. Jeannie held onto his hand as she looked at her doll. Mr. Wilson was behind the counter watching them. He was glad he was saving the special doll for Jeannie. Jeannie told the doll good-by as they left.

When they turned into the driveway at Grandpa's house, old Bones met them with a wagging tail. She had asked Grandpa about the dog's name. He had said.

"Old Bones was a stray when he wandered into the driveway here. He was nothing but skin and bones. Grandma and I felt sorry for him and fed him. He soon put some fat onto his bones, but the name Bones still seemed to fit him and he seemed to like it."

Jeannie had learned to walk by hanging onto old Bones. He watched over her whenever she played in the yard. Grandpa also has an old horse he calls, "Nellie." He used to farm with her, but now he just keeps her around for an old friend. He does give Jeannie a ride on her, which Jeannie and Nellie both enjoy. He had a hard time getting enough feed to feed her through the winter. A neighbor usually gives him a few bales of hay. Nellie survives on green grass in the pasture during the summer. Her teeth are worn now with age and Grandpa Fred does not know how much longer she can nibble grass.

The next afternoon Jeannie and her mom went to Mr. Wilson's toy store to sing Christmas carols. As her mom strummed her guitar, they both sang. People stopped by to listen to them and wandered into the store. Most of them left the store with a bag full of toys. Mr. Wilson would step out and listen whenever he got a chance. The cold north wind was blowing, but Jeannie and her mom bravely sang on to the people who stopped to listen. It worried Jeannie when she saw other girls looking at the doll in the window. Jeannie was chilled when they finished the first day, but she didn't mind. Four more days and the doll in the window would go home with her.

When they arrived home, Old Bones met them with a wag of the tail and a lick on their hands as they walked to the backdoor. Grandpa had hot soup made and was waiting for them. The next two days were cold enough to see their breath as they sang, but sing on they did. Again they were met by Old Bones and hot soup waiting for them. On the third day, Jeannie said to her grandpa.

"Grandpa, just two more days and the doll in the window is mine."

Grandpa smiled as he replied.

"Jeannie, I am so very proud of you. You are truly a little angel working to give that special doll a home and someone to love."

The next morning when Jeannie woke up and looked out of the window, she saw it was snowing and the wind was blowing. Grandpa did not want them to go sing, but they insisted. They only had to do it two more days before they could collect their pay. It had helped Mr. Wilson's business. As they drove down the country road going to town, they could see the snow starting to drift. Jeannie's mom hoped they would be able to get home after singing.

It snowed and the wind blew as they sang. When they were through, Mr. Wilson told them to stay in town. He had a place in the back of the store where they could stay. Jeannie's mom was worried about Grandpa Fred and said.

"We need to try to get home. I know Grandpa is worried and he will have a hot meal waiting for us."

It was a regular blizzard when they left Mr. Wilson's store. Grandpa had put car chains on the car before they left home. They became stuck in a huge snow drift less than a mile from home. It was snowing so hard it was causing a white out. Jeannie's mom knew they were low on gas and would freeze if they stayed in the car. They decided to walk the rest of the way.

Grandpa Fred had brought Old Bones into the house while he waited for his daughter and granddaughter. The temperature was below zero and there was a blizzard outside. He had the hot meal on the table. He sat and worried about his family. He waited and the soup got cold. He put it back in the pot on the stove to keep warm. He waited and waited. He wanted to go look for them. He tried to call Mr. Wilson's store but there was no answer. Finally, he put on his coveralls and along with Old Bones, went to the barn. He saddled old Nellie and left to look for his girls. He followed the fence row as Nellie struggled to get through the snow. He could not see over three feet in front of him. He just followed the fence.

When he found the car, it was empty. Any tracks the girls had left were now blown full of snow. Had they become lost? All he could do was turn Nellie around and follow the fence home. The neighbors found his family the next day. They had found them too late.

Mr. Wilson waited until a week after Christmas and the county had plowed the snow off the road. He picked up the doll in the window and slowly drove to Grandpa Fred's place. When he turned into the driveway, Old Bones met him with one bark. Mr. Wilson got out of his car with the doll. He walked to the front door and knocked. Grandpa Fred opened the door and invited him in. Mr. Wilson said.

"I brought the doll your granddaughter earned and the money your daughter earned. I am so sorry. I tried to get them to stay in town at my store, but they insisted on going home."

Grandpa Fred took the doll and thanked Mr. Wilson. Then he said.

"I thank you for saving the doll for Jeannie. She loved this little doll."

Grandpa Fred seemed to give up after that. The bill collectors took his home and what little farm land he had. They even took Old Nellie and sold her. He was now homeless but he still had Old Bones and Jeannie's doll. Bones and Grandpa Fred slept in the alleys or where ever they could find a place to rest and be out of the weather. One night just before Christmas, Grandpa Fred, Old Bones and three other homeless men were gathered around a barrel they were burning wood in to keep warm. Suddenly, Old Bones trotted off a few feet and looked down the dark alley. He gave one soft bark and started to wag his tail. The men listened and heard a guitar playing Christmas carols and sweet voices singing. Suddenly two angels appeared. One homeless man asked another.

"Who are they?"

The angels had been singing in front of Mr. Wilson's store. When they left he followed them. He had heard the question the homeless man had asked. He saw Grandpa Fred standing in the reflection of the flames in the barrel holding the doll that had been in the window. Grandpa Fred was so amazed he could not talk at first.

Mr. Wilson stepped forward to where the men could see him and he said.

"They are Grandpa Fred's daughter and Granddaughter."

Grandpa Fred then said.

"Jeannie, I have your doll and will take care of her until I come to see you at your new home."

That very night Grandpa Fred lay down in a big cardboard box with Old Bones to sleep. When his daughter and Little Jeannie went back to their new home they took Old Bones and Grandpa Fred with them.

Faded Plastic Flowers

WRITTEN BY
LLOYD WRIGHT

Faded Plastic Flowers

Granny was sitting on her enclosed front porch watching the colored fall leaves do their dance as they twirled through the air. The air was chilly outside, but the morning sun had warmed the porch. She did pull her shawl tighter as she enjoyed mother nature doing her annual ritual. The first frost had wilted some of her outdoor flowers and it did seem to make the pansies come to life. She let her eyes glance over to a bouquet of faded, plastic flowers sitting in a vase on a small stand in the corner of the porch. These flowers held more beauty, in her mind, than any flowers she had ever seen. She kept these flowers because they were so special and had touched her heart when she received them. A tear sneaked out of her eye and crawled down her cheek as she closed her eyes and let her mind drift back through time.

She recalled when her husband, Gramps, had volunteered to read to a kindergarten class. She had worked at an day care center before she retired and she felt she was ready to stay home and become a full time homemaker. She loved to bake and would bake cookies for the kindergarten class on a student's birthday. She would also help pick out gifts at Christmas time for the children and their teacher and wrap them. She was mainly a stay home partner and helped Gramps when he needed something special for the kindergarten class. After some coaxing, he had talked her into visiting the class on special occasions and read to the children.

When she did go to school, she enjoyed reading to the children very much. A little boy who sat in the front row seemed to attract her attention right away. She just felt something special toward this young lad. When she questioned Gramps about this student he replied.

"Your attention is direct to him because of your grandmotherly instincts. You knew he needed to give you the hugs he gives you and he needed the hugs you returned to him."

Every time she visited the class with Gramps she became more attached to all the students, but this one still caught her eye. Some of the children had never eaten a home made cookie, so she made a mental note to have ice cream and cookies there for the birthdays. She made sure she never missed going to school with Gramps on these days. She had received a lot of experience reading to the younger children at the day care and could easily keep the kindergarten children's attention. Gramps did his magic tricks for the children and played his harmonica and flute to entertain the class. He also had puppets, who would talk and sing. She left all that nonsense up to him. She stuck to reading children stories.

Gramps had written a story about a little dinosaur named Herbie who had no friends and he wanted to buy him tennis shoes, so he could run and jump without bothering anyone. He got the idea that maybe, this little fellow was hiding in the mountains so his so called friends would not see him cry. He used this idea for another story, which included taking a trip to the Grand Canyon and looking for Herbie. He asked her if she would like to take a trip to some national parks and look for Herbie. By writing this story he could help educate the children about this nation's great national parks. It took a lot of convincing, but finally she had agreed to accompany him on this trip. They were both retired so what was to keep them from sight seeing.

Gramps had told Mrs. Finch, the kindergarten teacher, about the planned trip toward the middle of May before school let out for the summer. He wanted her to know he would not be coming to school then, so she would not plan on him being there. Granny continued her trip down memory lane. She recalled that two days before they were ready to leave, Mrs. Finch called them and asked them to please visit the class the next day. The children wanted to see us one last time before we left. When we got back, school would be out for the summer. After some more coaxing, they had agreed to visit the children.

Granny recalled how the children were so happy to see them.

Unknown to Gramps and her, all the children had each brought them a going away gift. Gramps did not want any gift and said he was only visiting the children because he enjoyed it. The children came forward one at a time. Some gave them disposal cameras to take pictures on their trip. Other children gave them small photo books. She remembered the little boy sitting in the front row sitting there with his head down. After all the children had given them a gift except this one student, she watched as he got something out of his desk. With his head bowed down, he slowly approached her with his hand behind his little back. When he finally stood in front of her, he pulled his little hand out from behind his back. In his hand, he had a faded bouquet of plastic flowers. As he handed them to her he said.

"This is all I have to give you."

She had felt her heart pound as she took the flowers with a tear in her eye.

She had hugged him and said.

"They are beautiful. I will keep them forever."

Santa Claus And Little Toot

WRITTEN BY
LLOYD WRIGHT

Santa Claus And Little Toot

Santa had his boots off as he sat in his workshop with his feet propped up on a work bench. His feet felt like he had walked one hundred miles today. As he rested his feet he thought about Little Toot the Train. He had given Gramps a diesel train to bring kindergarten classes to visit the North Pole because Little Toot, the steam engine, burned coal and polluted the North Pole. Last year when Gramps gave Little Toot full throttle for take off, soot had covered everything, including Mrs. Claus and himself. He let Gramps know Little Toot could not return to the North Pole again. Santa sure would miss seeing and hearing the little train. He loved the sound of it's steam whistle as it approached the North Pole. Gramps always tooted it good-by as they disappeared in the Milky Way going home.

As Santa was in the middle of his trip down memory lane, Melrose, the Elf Magician, walked in to tell Santa about some new magic tricks he had packaged and was ready for Christmas presents. Children and adults alike wanted magic tricks for Christmas presents. Melrose could tell by the look on Santa's face that something was on his mind. Before he told Santa about the new magic tricks, he stopped and said.

"Santa, I can tell by the look on your face you have something on your mind."

Santa looked up at Melrose and replied.

"Melrose, you remember Little Toot the Train and Gramps. Little Toot was polluting the North Pole with the smoke from the stack on his engine. I gave Gramps a diesel engine and told him Little Toot could not come back. I want to invite Gramps and three kindergarten classes for a visit during their Christmas vacation like I have done in the past. Mrs. Claus mentioned them this morning while we were eating breakfast. I would like for Little Toot to bring these children to the North Pole, but

I just can't have his soot dirty this clean landscape. I will sure miss Little Toot and his steam whistle: it won't be the same without him."

Melrose looked at Santa as he smiled and said.

"Santa, I knew you liked Little Toot so I have been working on a way to make clean coal so he won't pollute. I have some magic powder you mix with the regular coal and it makes it burn clean."

Santa jumped up as he said.

"Hot dig-a-dee-dog Melrose, you have just made my Christmas. I'll have Wayne the Christmas Tree Elf stop by your workshop and pick some up. Would you also give him some of the magic powder so Little Toot can fly? He really enjoyed flying and so did Gramps."

Santa was pleased with the magic Melrose had packaged and made ready for Christmas. He had been receiving a lot of requests for magic tricks to give as gifts. Santa even planned to give Gramps some since he liked visiting the kindergarten classes and showing them magic. After Melrose left, Santa decided to have Matilda, the Elf Principal of the North Pole School system, take a trip and invite three kindergarten classes Gramps visits and the ladies from the elementary office to the North Pole during their Christmas vacation. These ladies had accompanied the children before and Mrs. Claus had told him to give them a special invitation.. She had missed their company and enjoyed their visit so very much. He had left it up to Gramps to talk to them before. Mrs. Claus wanted a special invitation given to them this year and she wanted Matilda to deliver it.

After Santa had sent Matilda on her special trip, he went looking for Wayne, the Christmas Tree Elf. He found Wayne at the North Pole Christmas candy shop. He was busy checking all the candy canes to be put on Christmas trees. Santa asked him to stop by Melrose's magic shop and pick up some magic powder to deliver to Gramps for Little Toot and invite him and Little Toot to bring the children for a Christmas visit. Tell Gramps he does not need to ask the teachers; Mrs. Claus told me to send Matilda with a special invitation for them. I asked her about a special invitation for Gramps and she said he did not need one. I know you are about ready to start your annual trip to check all the Christmas trees. Tell Gramps hello for me and to have Little Toot blow his steam whistle when they have the North Pole in sight.

When Wayne arrived at Gramps home, he found Gramps sleeping in his recliner and Little Toot sitting under the Christmas tree looking sad. Granny was in the kitchen making Christmas candy. After he had sampled Granny's candy, he crawled up in the Christmas tree to look it over. As he did, he knocked a Christmas tree bulb off hitting Little Toot on his caboose. The sound of the bulb breaking woke Gramps up. He smiled when he saw it was his old friend Wayne. Wayne asked Gramps.

"Where is the diesel engine Santa Claus gave you?"

Gramps replied.

"It is my den sitting under the Christmas tree I leave up all year for the Grandchildren. Little Toot has earned the place of honor to be under the big Christmas Tree."

Wayne then said.

"Little Toot should be happy instead of looking sad."

Gramps said.

"He is sad because he can not go back to the North Pole. He always enjoyed the trip and watching all the children as they played and rode in Santa's sleigh. He will miss that; I guess he is a little jealous being replaced by a diesel engine."

Wayne then told Gramps and Little Toot about his visit with Santa. He told them about the magic powder to make regular coal burn clean and the magic flying powder. He also wanted both of them to visit and bring three kindergarten classes. He also told him about Matilda so he would not have to ask the school staff and teachers about the North Pole trip. When Little Toot heard the conversation, he came alive and started circling the tree and tooting his steam whistle. Gramps said.

"Wayne, you just brought me the best news I have heard all year. Tell Santa we will be there and to listen for Little Toot's whistle."

Wayne finished inspecting Gramps tree and as he jumped down to leave, he grabbed a candy cane. Granny gave him two Christmas cookies to take along so he wouldn't starve to death on his trip back to the North Pole.

Matilda visited the school and received a welcome fit for a queen by Shelia King and Amber Stewart in the office. They received their special invitations and accepted right away. Mrs. Angie Middleton, the elementary principal, and Mrs. Tiffany Kennemore, the assistant elementary principal, gave Matilda a warm welcome and showed her around the school. They were given their special invitations and then they told Matilda to tell Mrs. Claus they were honored to receive a special invitation and were looking forward to visiting with her again.

Matilda visited the three kindergarten classes to extend Santa's invitation to visit the North Pole during their Christmas Vacation. She knew a note would have to be sent home with each student to get the parent's permission. She was introduced to each student while in their classroom. She was given a list of the teachers and students in each room to take to Mrs. Claus which read as follows;

KINDERGARTEN CLASSES

Mrs. Susan Keller	Miss Shanna Clark	Mrs. Laura Davis
Andreannah	Abigail	Will
Aniyah	Kaden	Kenzie
Arieyanna	Ryan	Layla
Ashley	Colton	Peyton
Belle	Charles	Yesenia
Devyn	Drew	Jose
Faythe	Ariana	Jadyn
Grayson	Kandes	Reid
Levi	Marshall	Marcus
Preston (P.J.)	Gabriela (Gabby)	Breiah
Raul	Kaitlyn	Mya
Rebecca	Devan	Taderian
Saige	Jayden	Allie

Shy'Kerria	Sara	Mekhi
Terassa	Larry	Richelle
Timothy	Connor	Logan
Xzavier	Marcus	Levi
		Mason

The teachers sent a note home with each of their students telling the parents about the North Pole invitation from Santa and Mrs. Claus and requesting permission for their children to go. Two days later all the permission notes were returned with all the students receiving permission. When Gramps visited the school he was informed all invitations had been accepted. He planned the route and made sure all necessary supplies would be on board Little Toot for the trip. He gave his plans for the trip and list of supplies to Mrs. Middleton for her approval. It was agreed to leave for the North Pole on the second day after Christmas vacation started.

On the morning of the scheduled departure, Gramps mixed the magic clean coal powder with the coal in the coal car. He then put the powder to fly in the boiler of Little Toot. He had enough for the round trip. He drank his coffee and ate a hearty breakfast. He knew it would be a long day for him as engineer and Little Toot. After breakfast and assuring Granny all was well, he bid her good-by with a kiss and climbed up into Little Toot's cab. They slowly chugged out of the driveway and turned toward the school.

When they chugged into the school parking lot, they found all the children anxiously waiting with their parents. They squeaked to a stop and all were ready to climb onboard. Miss Clark, Mrs. Davis, and Mrs. Keller called the roll for their students and counted heads as their student climbed aboard with the help of Amber Stewart and Shelia King. Mrs. Middleton and Mrs. Kennemore were going over all the supplies with Gramps in the Baggage, Dining, and Pullman cars. Gramps had already put the necessary Arctic clothing where the passengers could put them on when they needed it crossing Canada.

After all the good-bys had been said and all passengers were on board, Mrs. Middleton informed Gramps. Gramps climbed up into Little Toot's cab and slightly cracked the throttle. Little Toot answered with a chug and gave two toots with his steam whistle. The trip was underway. Gramps guided Little Toot toward the long runway on the Aeroplex located across the street from the school.

He had already filed the flight plan. When they arrived at the end of the runway, Gramps notified the control tower and requested permission to proceed onto the active runway. The tower gave him permission to proceed to runway three-zero. Gramps double checked the magic powder mix for the coal and flying. After Little Toot was lined up on the active runway, the control tower gave them permission to take off. Gramps opened Little Toot's throttle and reported to the tower they were rolling. As the throttle was being opened to full power, little fin like wings with ailerons and flaps extended from each side of Little Toot's engine and railcars. There was no black smoke pouring out of Little Toot's smoke stack. When Little Toot lifted off, Gramps notified the tower. The tower informed him to turn to a heading of three-six-zero and to climb to fifteen hundred feet. Gramps answered with.

"Roger tower, heading three-six-zero and climbing to fifteen hundred feet."

Gramps breathed a sigh of relief and set the throttle for climb power. They were finally on their way to visit Santa at the North Pole. The children watched the runway disappear and were all excited. The teachers pointed out the Mississippi River to their class and also informed them that the state across the river was Tennessee As they flew north, they saw the state of Missouri on one side of the river and Kentucky on the other. When the Ohio River was in sight, the teachers informed their students the Ohio River and Mississippi River were the rivers Huckleberry Finn rode his raft on during his adventure. The next state they saw was Illinois. When they flew over the City of Saint Louis, they saw the Arch of Saint Louis where the pioneers started their trek west. North of Saint Louis they saw the locks where the river traffic is raised and lowered by water level controlled by the locks. As they continued north, the children saw the state of Iowa where snow covered the corn stocks left in the fields after harvest. When the State of Wisconsin was below them, the teachers informed their classes that this state is a dairy state and known for making cheese. The State of Minnesota was far off to their left, but in sight.

Soon the border between Ontario Canada and the United States passed below them as Little Toot continued chugging along. The students had been watching the snow covered land below for moose. The farther north they traveled the shorter the daylight became. Some of the students had gone to the Pullman car for a nap and some were in the dining car having a snack with some hot chocolate and marshmallows. Gramps had warmed a can of soup on Little Toot's boiler and was enjoying it with a sandwich. He had Hudson Bay in sight. Little Toot had been traveling at a high speed. He was anxious to get his precious cargo to The North Pole.

The Northern Lights were playing in the sky, when they crossed into the Northwest Territories. Amber Stewart and Shelia King had put on their arctic gear and went forward to visit Gramps in the cab. They had helped the teachers with the children and all were settled in now for a nap. The last time they visited the North Pole, they had been in Little Toot's cab as he approached the North Pole. They had enjoyed the view so much they wanted to see the Northern Lights dance across the sky as they flew over the snow covered Arctic. When they crawled off of the coal car, Gramps welcomed them into the warm cab. He fixed them a hot cup of cocoa and told them if they got cold they could warm up by scooping some coal into Little Toot's firebox.

Santa had just finished eating and was walking to the barn to check on his reindeer, when he heard Little Toot's whistle. He had been waiting for that sound. He scurried back to the house to tell Mrs. Claus. He knew she would want to watch Toot land and pull into the long heated shed. She had already taken the list of children from Matilda and had them assigned to stay with the elf families. Santa and Mrs. Claus stood arm in arm as they watched the little train with its precious cargo appear out of the colorful swirling Milky Way. Santa was glad to see that Little Toot was leaving only a condensation trail and no soot trail from his smoke stack. Melrose's magic clean coal powder had worked.

Santa and Mrs. Claus could see smiling children's faces in the train windows as Little Toot made a smooth landing and slowly pulled into the heated train shed Santa had specially built for Toot. Santa and Mrs. Claus were impatiently waiting at the passenger car door to greet the children. As each child stepped off the train, they were swooped up in Mrs. Claus's arms receiving a great big welcoming hug. Santa stood right behind her and as she put each child down he swooped them up with a great big Santa welcoming hug and a cheerful Ho-Ho-Ho. Mrs. Middleton and her office staff received hugs along with the teachers by both Mrs. Claus and Santa. Mrs. Claus and Santa were thrilled to have visitors.

All the passengers were just leaving Little Toot, when Gramps walked up. When Gramps finally came walking toward them, Mrs. Claus stopped and gave him the same welcome as she had given the ladies. Santa shook his hand and then gave Gramps a huge bear hug. The elf men helped Santa and Gramps unload the luggage. The ladies were staying with the Claus' and the children had already been assigned to stay with elf families. Gramps had hooked up power to the railcars and would be residing in the Pullman car. Santa informed Gramps he would be eating up at the house with him. Not once did Gramps object to that.

Mrs. Claus along with the elf ladies had prepared a warm meal for their guest at the North Pole Community Center. After they had their fill of delicious food and desserts, the children were introduced to the families they were to stay with. The teachers and elf ladies accompanied the children to where they were to stay. The children fell in love with the houses and the furnishings. They were made for small people just like them. After the teachers had insured each of their students were well taken care for the night, they went to see Mrs. Claus and unpacked their suitcases. As they rested after a long trip, the ladies sat around the kitchen table exchanging news while they sipped on hot drinks and nibbled on snacks. Gramps and Santa brought each other up to date on the news happenings at the North Pole and the outside world. This was of course between short snoozes and snores.

The next morning the children ate breakfast with the elves they were guests of Mrs. Claus along with the help of the ladies, fixed a huge breakfast. After all were seated, Santa blessed the meal and then dove into a plate heaping full of hot biscuits and gravy. The plates of food were soon emptied as they were passed around. Santa and Gramps did their share of emptying. They had a choice of hot coffee, tea, or chocolate. After all were finished eating Santa took his napkin and wiped the excess gravy from his beard.

As the breakfast table was being cleared by the ladies, Santa and Gramps got out of their way and went to the barn to check on the reindeer and hold a bale of hay down. Mrs. Claus knew the teachers were anxious about the students so she suggested they check up on them while the dishes were being washed. There would not be enough room for all to help anyway. The teachers found the students were being well taken care of. It had already been planned for Mrs. Keller's students to visit Toyland, Mrs. Davis's students to ride in Santa's sleigh through the Milky Way, and Miss Clark's students to visit the barn and reindeer during the morning. In the afternoon, they would exchange places to visit and the following morning exchange again so all students get to visit the same places.

When Santa arrived at the barn, he found Rufus feeding the reindeer. After Rufus was through Santa had him harness the work reindeer and hitch them to the passenger sleigh. He had decided to use the work reindeer so his regular reindeer he used on Christmas Eve would be well rested. They had a long trip ahead of them. When Mrs. Davis's class arrived at the reindeer barn Santa was ready to take them for a ride through the Aurora Borealis, which is also known as the Northern Lights. She had her class line up and then she said.

"As I call your names, Santa and Gramps will help you get into the sleigh: Will, Kenzie, Layla, Peyton, Yesenia, Jose, Jadyn, Reid,

Marcus, Breiah, Mya, Taderian, Allie, Mekhi, Richelle, Logan, Levi, and Mason.

After all were on board and secured, Mrs. Laura Davis was told to sit up front with Santa so they could visit and she could drive the reindeer through the swirling lights if she wanted to. The children were all snug and excited as they heard Santa say.

"Now Brutus, Now Cletus, Now Ethyl, and John, up, up and away."

The trip through the colorful lights had begun and it would be a sight the class would never forget.

Miss Shanna Clark arrived at the reindeer barn just in time to see the sleigh and reindeer take off with their friends. They were met at the barn door by Gramps and Rufus. The class was divided into two groups. Abigail, Kaden, Ryan, Colton, Charles, Drew, Ariana, and Kandes went with Rufus the oldest elf and took turns riding on a reindeer that used to be a saddle horse. Marshall, Gabby, Kaitlyn, Devan, Jayden, Sara, Larry, Conner, and Marcus along with Miss Clark followed Gramps up into the hayloft. There they found Mrs. King and Mrs. Stewart were already there swinging on the hay rope. They helped Miss Clark as the children would swing on the rope and drop onto the hay below. The children all watched as their teacher took her turn.

As Mrs. Susan Keller and her students were going to Toyland, they heard the children in the barn laughing. They were anxious to visit Toyland but were also anxious to fly through the swirling colorful lights and to play in the barn. When they arrived at Toyland they were met by an old elf cowboy called, Wyoming. He took them on a tour of Toyland riding in a stage coach pulled by six magic horses. When the tour was finished he said.

"You can help make whatever Christmas presents you choose."

Mrs. Keller listened as her students told Rufus where they would like to help. Xzavier, Timothy, and Raul wanted to work where they made videos games. Teressa, Shy'Kerria, Saige, and Belle, chose to help make dolls. Adreannah, Aniya, Arieyanna, Ashley, Faythe and Rebecca chose to help Melrose and his elf helpers make magic gifts. Devin,

Grayson, Levi, and Preston (P.J.), saw where the four wheelers were made and wanted to help there.

Everyone met at the community center for the noon meal. After they were all seated, Santa looked out over the tables and saw rosy cheeked children. He could readily see they had a busy and enjoyable morning. Santa bowed his head and said a Prayer of Thanks. The food rapidly disappeared from the table and into hungry stomachs, including Santa. During the afternoon, the classes exchanged activities. Mrs. Davis's class visited Toyland, Mrs. Keller's class visited the reindeer barn, and Miss Clark's class enjoyed the scenery as they rode through the northern lights. Tomorrow morning they would exchange again thus giving all a chance to visit the same places.

After a busy afternoon, they met at the North Pole Community Center for the evening meal. Santa looked out over the tables loaded with food and saw red faced tired children. They had been busy all day. Santa said Grace and then the food started to disappear. Gramps sat by Santa and marveled at how much he could eat. Of course, Gramps ate his share also. The desserts consisted of different hot cobblers and ice cream to cool it down with. After the evening meal, the children gathered on the stage and sang Christmas Carols. The elf families had joined in the evening meal and enjoyed listening to the children sing. The evening was soon over and it was time for a good nights rest for all.

The next morning the children ate breakfast with the families they were staying with and the ladies and Gramps ate with Santa and Mrs. Claus. Santa again had his biscuits and gravy and washed it down with coffee. Gramps settled for a couple of biscuits with gravy and also a couple pancakes. Mrs. Claus had arisen early and made a coffee cake for dessert. After the meal, Santa took his napkin and wiped his beard. Santa and Gramps got out of the ladies way and scurried off toward the barn. When they went in the barn, they found Rufus had already fed the reindeer, so they found a bale of hay to hold down as they rested their stomachs.

Rufus harnessed the work team reindeer and hitched them to the passenger sleigh. Mrs. Keller and her class were soon in the passenger sleigh and ready for a ride through the swirling lights. After all were settled and secured in, they heard Santa speak softly to his reindeer saying.

"Now Brutus, Now Cletus, Now, Ethyl, and John, up, up, and away."

They were soon airborne and enjoying the beautiful rainbow colors as they flew through them.

Mrs. Davis and her class were enjoying the activities in the barn. Some rode the old reindeer that used to be a saddle horse, while the others catapulted off the hay rope into the hay below. Everyone had their turn in the hayloft and riding the reindeer. The ladies waited until they thought no one was watching and then they all had a swing on the hay rope.

Miss Clark's class toured Toyland, escorted by Wyoming, the old elf cowboy. The students then told Wyoming they would like to help make Christmas gifts. After they were all busy, Miss Clark walked through Toyland checking on her class. She took the time to work a while with each one making gifts. The morning passed too quickly for everyone. They again gathered at the North Pole Community Center for lunch, which again was plentiful and disappeared quickly. After lunch, Santa and Gramps watched the children as they tried ice skating in the indoor ice skating rink. The children were amazed how graceful Santa was on ice skates. Rufus and Wyoming gave some of the children rides on snow mobiles. The teachers, along with the office staff, visited the North Pole School. Matilda introduced them to all of her staff and teachers. Then the ladies checked on the children and tried ice skating also. When the afternoon was over, all were sore and tired. Tomorrow they had to return home. All the visitors, Santa, Mrs. Claus, and all the elf families gathered for the evening meal which was abundant. After all were seated, Santa stood up and said a special prayer for all those present and all the people around this great big world. After the prayer the food again disappeared quickly. Santa said a silent prayer for all the children around the world who would be going to bed hungry tonight while they feasted. It just did not seem fair to him. Maybe he could somehow help the children around the world this Christmas.

After the evening meal was done, all the children including the elf children gathered on the stage and sang Christmas carols. As all their voices joined in unison, Santa and Mrs. Claus both felt a chill run up their backs. They had truly enjoyed every moment with their visitors. After the children were all tucked in bed, the ladies gathered in the living room with Mrs. Claus and visited. She did get lonely sometimes and had looked so forward to their visit. The time had passed so quickly.

Santa and Gramps strolled under the northern lights talking and checking around to make sure all was well. Santa and Gramps crawled up in Little Toot's cab and sat there for a long time just visiting. They both loved children and both wished they could do more for them. The time did come for them to get some rest; they both had a long day ahead of them. Gramps and Little Toot would be making the journey home and Santa would be checking and double checking his list and overseeing the loading of his sleigh for the long journey he would be making. Santa walked with Gramps to the Pullman car and bid each other good night. Gramps climbed up into the car as Santa trudged to his house softly humming a Christmas carol.

Everyone woke up early and gathered to have breakfast together. Gramps advised all the children to eat a hearty meal because they were going home today. After all were seated, Santa stood up and bowed his head. He asked the food be blessed they were about to receive. He asked that his guests have a safe journey home. He closed his prayer asking for world peace so all the children in the world could have a warm bed to sleep in and a hot meal served to them with love.

After all had eaten their fill, the visitors gathered by Little Toot to climb onboard. The elves loaded the luggage along with special gifts Santa had given to each guest. The teachers called their class roll and counted heads, and then they were given a hug by Mrs. Claus and Santa before they climbed the steps. After all the good-bys had been said and hugs given, all the guest climbed aboard Little Toot. Gramps thanked Santa and Mrs. Claus for their kindness and generosity. Gramps shook

Santa's hand and hugged Mrs. Claus before he walked to Little Toot's engine.

When Mrs. Middleton told Santa to signal Gramps all were on board and ready, Gramps cracked the throttle slightly and backed out onto the runway. Little Toot gave two toots on his whistle as Gramps opened the throttle for takeoff power. Santa was sad they were leaving and glad that Little Toot did not pollute the North Pole with black soot. The children were waving as Little Toot gathered speed and lifted off into the northern lights. Shelia King and Amber Stewart could be seen waving from Little Toot's caboose. They wanted to watch as they flew through the Northern Lights. Gramps set the climb power and Little Toot tooted a long good-by as they disappeared in the Aurora Borealis. When their cruising altitude was reached, he set the auto pilot and cruise power. They were headed home to anxious parents.

Christmas Tree In A Window

WRITTEN BY
LLOYD WRIGHT

Christmas Tree In A Window

The children on the school bus noticed a small, run down house along the bus route with a little Christmas tree by a front window. The only decorations on the tree was a little star hanging down at the top and a string of lights with only four lights shining. On the days it was nice outside, a little old lady sat on the front porch with a worn and torn shawl wrapped around her shoulders. She would smile and wave as long as the bus was in sight. Everyday the children looked with interest at the sparsely decorated Christmas tree and all would wave to the lady when she was outside. When the weather was bad she could be seen looking out of the front window by the Christmas tree. Two kindergarten students watched for the lady everyday and decided to tell their teacher about the Christmas tree and the lady. They wished they could help her.

The two kindergarten students approached the teacher's desk one morning. Mrs. Williams, their teacher, noted the troubled look on their faces. They told her about the little old lady and the Christmas tree with very little decorations on it. They wanted to help her but did not know how to. Mrs. Williams had been trying to find a Christmas project for her class. Mrs. Thompson, another kindergarten teacher, had told her she was looking for a Christmas project also. She would talk to her and see if they could take this little old lady as their Christmas project to help. First, she had to find out more about this lady and the Christmas tree.

That very afternoon she asked for and was given permission to ride on the school bus with the children. She informed the bus driver why she was a passenger. He knew the lady and offered to introduce Mrs. Williams and Mrs. Thompson to her the following week-end. Her name is Mrs. Emily Hopper. She likes to be called Emma. When the bus approached Mrs. Hopper's house, she was sitting on the front porch smiling and waving. Mrs. Williams knew at that very moment she had found the Christmas project for her class, thanks to the compassion of two of her students. She made arrangements with the bus driver to go to Mrs. Hopper's home Saturday afternoon.

The bus driver met Mrs. Williams and Mrs. Thompson in front of Mrs. Hopper's home. They knocked on the front door and were greeted by a smiling little old lady. He bus driver introduced Mrs. Hopper to the teachers. She invited them in to visit. She was always pleased to have company visit. After they were seated, Mrs. Hopper apologized for not having any refreshments to serve. She went on and said.

"A tornado destroyed our home three years ago. I lost my husband and everything we owned. I did find my little Christmas tree and a string of lights in the debris. As you can see, it isn't much but that little tree is special to me."

Mrs. Hopper took a corner of her worn apron and wiped a tear from her eye, which had crept out.

Mrs. Williams said.

"Mrs. Hopper."

Mrs. Hopper interrupted her as she said.

"Please call me Emma."

Mrs. Williams said.

"Emma, Mrs. Thompson kindergarten class, along with my class would like to sing Christmas carols to you one evening. The children see you wave when they ride on the school bus by here and would like to meet you. Two of my students think you would make a perfect granny for the class and would like for you to visit our classroom."

Emma thought for a moment and replied.

"I would love to meet the children and hear them sing Christmas carols. My husband and I were never blessed with children. Christmas is my favorite time of the year. I will always remember as a child how excited I would be on Christmas Eve waiting for Santa Claus."

Emma showed the teachers her little Christmas tree sitting on a table in front of the window. Four lights were twinkling just as Emma's eyes were.

When it came time to leave, Emma did not want her guests to leave. She enjoyed their company very much. She stood in the doorway and waved until they were out of sight.

The teachers decided to have the children sing the same Christmas carols they had been practicing for their Christmas program. The children loved to sing. Every day they practiced singing, Jingle Bells, Oh Christmas Tree, Let It Snow, Go Tell it on the Mountain, Rudolph, Upon The House Top, Silent Night, and We wish You a Merry Christmas. A note was sent home with each student telling the parents about the plans to sing Christmas carols to Mrs. Hopper. The note also mentioned a little ornament for her tree and permission for their children to attend. When the notes returned to the teachers, they found all the students had been given permission. Three of the fathers had volunteered to winterize Mrs. Hopper's house. Two notes told how two fathers would pay Mrs. Hopper's gas and electric bills for the month of December.

The students wanted to give Mrs. Hopper something for her tree. Mrs. Williams and Mrs. Thompson had already decided to give Emma a new shawl and apron. The teachers asked each of their students.

"What would you like to give Mrs. Hopper for her tree?"

Mrs. Williams class responded as follows:

Emily - A candy cane.
Elizha - A Santa Claus ornament.
Trinity - A kitty-cat ornament.
Jae'lyn - A teddy bear ornament.
Brayden - A ginger bread wreath.
Elizabeth - Another string of lights.
Hunter G. - A glass ball ornament.
Abigail (Abby) - A princess ornament.
Serenity - A heart ornament.
William - A blue ball ornament.
Skylen - An apple ornament.
Clarence - A gingerbread man ornament.
Kenneth - Star ornament.

John - A box of ornaments.
Sylvia - A turkey ornament.
Jaden (J.J.) - Plastic candy cane.
Hunter B. - A gingerbread boy ornament.
Brock - A butterfly ornament.

Mrs. Thompson's class responded as follows:
Jordan - Christmas lights and coffee cup.
Reese - A cat ornament.
Keely - Candy canes
Rylee - Candy canes.
Jenna - A star.
Kayleen - Christmas tree lights.
Destiny - Ornaments.
Randall - A tree skirt.
Arianna - Lights.
Tara - A snowman ornament.
Gage - Lights.
Juan - A snowman ornament.
Carly - A sun ornament.
Ashton - Ornament.
Tristan - Candy canes.
Charles - A Santa Claus ornament.
Seth - A Santa Claus ornament.

Mrs. Hopper was sitting in her rocking chair close to the heating stove. She had the worn shawl wrapped around her shoulders. It had snowed a little today, just enough to turn the ground a clean white. It had stopped in the middle of the afternoon and the sky cleared to a deep blue. The moon light was reflecting off the snow making it light as day outside. She closed her eyes as she felt the warmth of the house making her drowsy. Three men had came to visit her last Saturday and winterized her house while they were there. She no longer could feel a cold draft around her windows or doors. She offered to pay them from her meager savings, but all they would accept was a smile, hug, and a thank you. Two men stopped by last Sunday after church and told her they had paid her electric and gas bill in advance for the month. They wished her a Merry Christmas as they left.

As Emma slowly rocked, she thought her mind was playing tricks on her. She thought she heard the voices of Angels singing. She opened her eyes and listened closely. She could hear children singing Jingle Bell. She got up from her rocker and walked over to the window by her Christmas tree. She peered out and saw her front yard full of children singing Christmas carols. She pulled her shawl tighter and opened the front door and stepped out on the porch. She never felt the cold; the warmth she felt when she heard and saw the children was enough to keep her warm.

The teachers stepped forward and placed a new warm shawl around Emma's shoulders. They handed her a gift wrapped in Christmas paper. The children along with their parents caroled Mrs. Hopper. When they finished singing, the teacher told Mrs. Hopper each of the children had a small gift for her to place on her Christmas tree. They asked her to step in the house and could one of them accompany her. They did not want the children to track up her house. Emma stepped inside and watched as the children came forward one at a time and handed her their gift. As she received each one, she gave each student a thank you with a hug.

After she had received all the gifts, the teachers helped Mrs. Hopper put the gifts on her tree as the children watched through the front window. After the last gift was placed on the tree, the children sang Oh Christmas Tree. Mrs. Hopper had tears in her eyes as the parents gave her a month's supply of groceries. When all the gifts had been given, the children sang We Wish You a Merry Christmas. Mrs. Hopper stood and watched as the children left with their parents. She had so much to be thankful for. When the children were out of sight, Emma stepped back into her cozy house and shut the door. She walked over to her rocking chair and sat down. She started softly humming Christmas carols as she admired her beautifully decorated Christmas Tree. Some of the ornaments the children had made themselves, which made them so special.

She Always Wore House Slippers

Written By
Lloyd Wright

She Always Wore House Slippers

Bailey sat at her kindergarten desk in deep thought. The teacher had given each student in her class paper to write a letter to Santa Claus on. There were so many things she wanted. She wanted a bicycle, roller skates, electronic games to play on the television, dolls, a doll stroller, and a new leash and collar for her dog she named Troubles. He had chewed on his leash and had outgrown his dog collar. She would even like to have a little four wheeler. She chewed the eraser off of her pencil while she was trying to make the right decisions. Finally, she let out a sigh and wrote down on the paper all she wanted was a new pair of house slippers for Mrs. Barker, the old lady who lives next door.

She had not told her mom and dad but her six month old dog had dug a hole under the chain link fence in her back yard and paid the lady a visit. He had found her house slippers she wore when she worked in her back yard on her back porch. They were big floppy slippers with a big flower sewed on each one. They used to have flowers until Troubles chewed them off. When her mom and dad had bought her a six weeks old puppy after she had nagged them a lot, she had made a promise that if they got her a dog she would be very responsible. If he damaged anything by chewing on it, she would have to take her allowance money and replace it. Her dad had made her promise that. She hated giving up what she wanted for Christmas, but she had spent all of her allowance money at the candy store.

Mrs. Barker is a nice old lady. She always speaks to her when she sees her outside playing with Troubles. She even sits with her and her brother when her parents go away in the evening. Bailey had never seen Mrs. Barker wear anything on her feet but house slippers. Some of her house slippers looked old and worn out, but she wore them anyway. She had asked her dad why the lady next door always wore house slippers.

He did not know why. She recalled when one day she saw Mrs. Barker working in her flower beds; she had climbed over the fence to go visit her. Mrs. Barker had continued digging around her flowers and putting a spray on them. Bailey remembers asking her.

"Why do you talk and sing to your flowers when you are working?"

She had replied.

"Young lady, flowers get lonely just like I do. It makes them happy when I talk and sing to them and it makes me happy. Don't singing make you happy? We keep each other company. I take care of my flowers and they give me happiness when I smell their sweetness, or they give me a bouquet to keep me company in the house."

Bailey watched Mrs. Barker work that day and asked her a million questions but never asked the all important one. Finally, when Mrs. Bailey stood up she groaned and then took a minute to straighten her back up. She walked over to her chair on the porch. She had said.

"Bailey, I am thirsty for something cold to drink. I think we can find something in the refrigerator for us to drink."

When she pulled off her old dirty garden slippers to put on her clean house slippers, Bailey saw the most awful looking toes and red swollen feet she had ever seen. She asked.

"What is wrong with your feet?"

Mrs. Bailey smiled and replied.

"I have arthritis in my feet and my toes are bent. I went to a foot doctor and he told me I had hammer toes. I can not wear shoes because they hurt my feet."

That was the day she had found out why Mrs. Bailey wore house slippers all the time.

Bailey read her letter to Santa and then showed it to her teacher. Her teacher put it in an envelope addressed to Santa Claus at the North Pole. She took the letter home and gave it to her mom to mail since she did not have money for the postage and could not reach the mail box.

Santa read the letter with a smile and then gave the letter to the elf responsible for filling the orders for him. Santa had told him to give her some presents that most young ladies want for Christmas along with a pair of big floppy ladies house slippers with a big flower on each of them.

When Bailey jumped out of bed on Christmas morning and ran down stairs, she was surprised to find she had several presents with her name on them. When she opened them she had received roller skates, a new doll, doll clothes, a electronic game, and a new pair of big floppy house slippers with a big flower on each one. The house slippers were too big for her. She looked at the card on the paper she had tore off the box. It had written on it: "To Bailey and Mrs. Barker from Santa." She rewrapped the box as good as she could. She found a bicycle in the garage from Santa when she was going outside through the garage to take a present to Mrs. Barker. Troubles went with her wearing a new collar and she had him on a new leash.

Bailey stepped onto Mrs. Barker's porch and rang the door bell. When Mrs. Barker opened the door she saw little red cheeked Bailey holding a Christmas package that had showed signs of being already opened and then rewrapped. Bailey handed her the gift as she said.

"Mrs. Barker, Troubles chewed the flowers off of your house slippers you wear outside to work in; I never told you he was the one who did it. I asked Santa to bring you a new pair."

Mrs. Barker took the package and opened it. She loved the new house slippers. She thanked Bailey with a hug as Troubles watched and wagged his tail. She said.

"Bailey this is the best present I have ever received from Santa and a little Angel."

I Heard
Animals Singing

WRITTEN BY
LLOYD WRIGHT

I Heard Animals Singing

Bobby stood on the school stage, practicing for his class Christmas play. He loved to sing but today his mind was elsewhere. His best friend Tommy had came over to his house after school yesterday and they made plans to go hunting when school got out today. They had both asked their dads to take them hunting, but they both always received the same reply.

"You are too young to go hunting. You are not big enough to even shoot a gun."

They each had a BB gun, but they could only target practice when their dads were with them. They planned on going hunting with their BB guns even if they did not have any BBs. Bobby met Tommy outside the school when school was out for the day. It was cold and getting colder but they didn't care as long as they could go hunting. They ran home and put on their camouflage hunting clothes. As Bobby was running toward the front door, his mom stopped him and asked.

"Where do you think you are going young man?"

Bobby said.

"Tommy and I are going hunting."

She had seen them hunt all the time in the backyard before so she told him.

"Just be careful and be in this house before dark. There is a blizzard heading this way and it is supposed to be here tonight."

Tommy was waiting outside for Bobby with his bicycle. Bobby got his bicycle out of the garage. He wanted to take his dad's hunting dog but he knew he couldn't. His dad had gotten Singing Sam when he was a puppy. He called him Singing Sam because he sure could sing when he was tracking game. He had a great nose and was the best when it came to tracking. They headed for the woods located just at the edge of town. They laid their bicycles down by the edge of the woods and pretended to load their empty guns.

The wind was blowing and the air was getting colder by the minute but they never noticed. Tommy saw a tree he wanted to sit by to watch for deer or whatever came by. Bobby said.

"If you shoot something just yell. I am going on into the woods just a little farther. My mom wants me home before it gets dark."

Bobby walked on into the woods for a little while. He sat down by a tree and looked around. He thought he saw something move farther on in the woods. He took his gun and crept ahead to see what it was. He saw a squirrel scamper up a tree and jump from tree top to tree top. He crept along following. When he did stop and look around, everything looked the same. He did not know the way back out of the woods. He yelled for his friend but no answer. It was getting colder and the sky was getting darker. He started running back toward where he thought his friend Tommy was at, but he never found him. Panic set in and he ran until he was exhausted. It was now dark in the woods.

He crawled up next to a big tree and cried. He was scared and exhausted from running. It started to snow and the wind blew harder. He thought he heard singing. He listened closely; maybe it was the wind blowing through the trees. Then he heard it again. He stood up and tried to follow the sound. It sounded like somebody or something was singing Christmas carols. He followed the sound until he was too tired to go on. He was cold and sleepy. He curled up in a pile of leaves next to a big tree. He did not want to close his eyes but he was so sleepy.

Later in the night he opened his eyes and saw forest animals all around him singing Christmas carols just like he had been practicing that very day at school. He saw a wild pig, three deer, a red fox, four coyotes, two wolves, a possum, two raccoons and a big black bear. The black bear was standing on a stump and directing the animals just like his teacher did at school practicing for the Christmas play. Bobby was so sleepy, but he no longer felt the cold.

Tommy waited for Bobby to come back out of the woods. He had been yelling his name but no answer. Finally it was getting dark and he knew he had to go home. When Tommy walked into his house his mom said.

"Tommy, where have you been? You should have been home before it got dark. It is too cold for you to be wandering around the neighborhood."

Tommy never said a word about Bobby because he knew he would be in trouble. He washed his hands and face and ate the evening meal with his family. As they were eating dessert, the telephone rang. His mom answered the phone and then he knew it was Bobby's mother calling to see if he was there. Bobby mom then said.

"Bobby told me he was going hunting with Tommy. I thought they were playing in the backyard here or at your house. Is Tommy home?"

When Tommy was questioned he had to admit he had left his friend in the woods.

Bobby's parents drove to the edge of the woods and found Bobby's bicycle but no Bobby. They called the Sheriff's office for help to look for their son. It was below zero by this time. Bobby's mom went home and sat by the telephone for any news as her husband and several men searched for Bobby. At midnight they still had not located him. Bobby's dad said to the other searchers.

"I am going home and get Singing Sam. He just may be able to find him although the chances are slim. The scent is cold and the ground is snow covered."

He returned a short time later with his dog. He held him on the leash and let him smell Bobby's dirty school shirt. He turned him loose where they had found the bicycle as he said.

"Find Bobby Singing Sam. I know you and him are the best of friends."

Sam wagged his tail as he searched the snow covered ground. About the time everyone watching thought they were too late, Singing Sam let out a yodel and started trailing into the woods as he stuck his nose through the snow and down into the leaves.

Bobby could hear a new voice added to the choir. A dog had joined in the singing of Christmas Carols. The big black bear walked over to

Bobby and picked him up. The bear held him close to his chest and covered him with his winter coat of hair as he carried him through the woods.

The next thing Bobby saw was his mom's face. He barely whispered.

"I heard animals singing. A big bear was there and picked me up and carried me."

Through tears Bobby's mom said.

"Just rest Bobby you are safe now. You are in a hospital."

After Bobby closed his eyes and went back to sleep, the doctor could see the puzzled look on Bobby's parent's face. He said.

"Bobby will recover just fine. He was suffering from loss of body temperature and hallucinating. It is a miracle he is alive. He was not clothed enough to withstand sub-zero temperatures. The animals he heard and saw singing Christmas Carols had to be a choir of angels looking over him. The dog he heard singing was your dog and the bear that picked him up and carried him to safety wrapped in a heavy coat was his dad."

Bobby's mom looked at her husband and said.

"Singing Sam is going to receive a very special Christmas present from me and the big old bear I am married too."

Arkansas Red Cedar Tree

Written By
Lloyd Wright

Arkansas Red Cedar Tree

Leonard lives on a farm with his three sisters and four brothers. Three of his brothers are older than him, which makes his growing up a little rough. They like to see if they can get him in trouble whenever they can. When it comes to fighting with the neighbor boys they stick together as a family. Fights were few and far between because their dad kept them out of trouble by keeping them busy helping on the farm. Leonard was always called Lonnie, and that is the name which stuck with him when he grew to be an adult.

When Lonnie was five years old, he was given certain chores to do. These chores had to be done every day, seven days a week. The animals must be taken care of, as well as the family seven days a week so daily chores never took a day off. The chores he was given was to gather the eggs in the chicken house nest every evening. The chickens must be fed and watered both morning and evening. He pumped water from the well and carried the water into the kitchen for drinking both morning and evening. He had to keep the wood box by the kitchen stove full so his mom could cook. His dad and older brothers cut the wood and he had to carry it in from the woodpile. He milked one old gentle cow both morning and evening. If he smelled like barnyard when he went to school, no one noticed. Even the teacher was a farm lady.

Now with all that said, the chore he dreaded doing every day was gathering eggs. Sometimes an old hen would be sitting on the nest and did not want to give up her egg. When Lonnie reached under her he would receive a pecking he would never forget. Once the eggs were gathered, he then had to journey to the farm house carrying the basket of eggs. Trouble was always waiting outside of the hen house door in the form of an old mean rooster. The minute he saw Lonnie the chase was on. If he caught him, he would fly up and not only peck him on the backside, but spur him with his spurs, which are sharp.

This is where the Arkansas Red Cedar Tree comes into the story. It is half way between the chicken house and the farm house. Lonnie would run as hard as his little legs would carry him to the tree. He spent a lot of time in this tree every day getting away from the rooster. He also played in it during the day, climbing and swinging on its branches. He grew to love and respect the tree. When the old rooster would get tired of waiting for him to come down out of the tree and leave, Lonnie would wait a while longer. He would then jump down and pick up the basket of eggs and try to beat the old rooster to the house. Sometimes he did and sometimes he didn't.

When Lonnie played in the cedar tree, he thought he could hear soft music playing. Sometimes the tree would whisper to him as he relaxed in its shade and just did nothing, except watch out for the rooster. He wished his mom would make chicken and dumplings out of the rooster and told his dad as such. His dad said.

"Son, that old rooster has chores to do on the farm, too. He chases you because he thinks you are carrying off his family. He also does it to keep in shape so he can wake up early and crow to tell us it is time to get up. If you watch him, he will tell us when something is just not right in the chicken house. Sometimes wild animals try to sneak in at night and hurt his girls. He will fight to the finish to protect them."

After a storm one night, Lonnie noticed a branch broken on the cedar tree. He could see where the wood was red on the inside. He decided to ask his dad why the wood was red. Lonnie's dad always had time for his family. He may keep working as he talked but he would always answer their curiosities. He thanked his son for pointing out the broken limb. He went to the tool shed and got his hand saw and sawed the limb off. He then said.

"Son, we will keep this broken limb until it dries then we will make something out of it. If you smell the fresh wood where it was cut, you will smell a fragrance you will never forget. The reason the wood is red inside is because the Arkansas Red Cedar Trees are keeping a promise.

Someday in school you will read about the Trail Of Tears. The story you read will not tell you about the Arkansas Red Cedar Tree, so it is up to us to tell the story to our children and for them to pass the story on.

There lived the Cherokee Indians in the southeastern United States. A little Cherokee girl grew up there among the cedar trees. When she was a baby they hung a little hammock on one of the cedar trees. As the southern breeze gently blew through the branches, it would rock her ever so gentle and sing a wind song to hear. She was named Songbird because she sang as soon as she could talk. The cedar tree loved this little girl and she loved the tree. When she grew into a young lady and had children of her own, they also swung on the cedar tree's branches as it rocked them gentle and sang them the wind song.

The white man wanted the land the Indians lived on and decided to make all the Cherokee Indians move to the Indian Territory, which is now the state of Oklahoma. It was a long distance to travel and they were force marched from their homeland to this territory. Many of Songbird's family and friends died on the way. The ground was stained along the way from those fighting for their life and freedom. The cedar tree cried in the wind and told how its' friends, the Cherokees were being treated and driven from their land. The message was passed from tree to tree all the way to the Indian Territory.

When Songbird arrived in Arkansas there had been so many of the tribe lost due to sickness and fatigue. The trail they followed became known as the Trail Of Tears. Songbird camped under an old Arkansas Cedar Tree the first night in Arkansas. The old cedar tree listened as she cried and told it about the hardships her people were enduring. The old tree had received the cedar tree's messages on the wind along the trail and knew of the hardships. Songbird listened to the wind song in the old tree as she wept that night. She asked the old cedar tree to remember the Cherokee and the tears, which were being shed and tell their story. The old tree promised with a whisper to her in the breeze that all the cedar trees would remember them. The old cedar tree asked all the other cedar trees to gather the Cherokee blood that had been shed and collect it from the stained ground with their roots and store it inside every branch and trunk. That is how the Arkansas Cedar Tree became known as the Arkansas Red Cedar Tree. This is also why all cedar trees have a reddish color inside.

Old Indians have taken the dead branches from the cedar trees and made red cedar flutes. It took a lot of time and patience. They had to use hot coals to burn the holes in the branch to make their Indian flutes. Sharpened rocks were used to fashion part of the flute. When they were finished, they would raise the flute to their lips and play a mournful tune on the wind, which told the tale of the Trail Of Tears. Songbird's request of the old cedar tree in Arkansas and its promise to her was never forgotten. You must remember this story and pass it along to your children someday. Your great, great grandmother was a full blooded Cherokee Indian lady. The red you see in the Arkansas Red Cedar tree is the same as yours."

After the branch dried that Lonnie's dad had cut from the tree, his dad showed him how to make train whistles and a small Indian flute. He also made candle holders. All the branch was used and not a piece was left to go to waste. He then said to Lonnie.

"Son, if you listen as you go through life you will hear music and voices coming from all cedar trees you encounter throughout your life's journey."

Lonnie never forgot what his dad had told him. He always respected the Arkansas Red Cedar Tree. When ever he saw one lying by the road to be chipped up he would approach the owner and ask for the tree. From those trees he renewed their lives by making all his children and grandchildren a cedar chest. All of them have in their possession an Arkansas Red Cedar Flute. He plays the flute he has everywhere he travels in this great country. The sound of his flute is helping keep the promise made years ago to Songbird. He hopes she is somewhere she can hear it.

Lonnie never forgot his trips to the hen house to gather the eggs and the old rooster. He loves to hold his grandchildren on his lap and tell them about his farm chores. The old wood box and wood burning kitchen stove are now just a memory, but he can still taste his mom's meals she cooked on the stove. He recalls to them how all the family and friends drank from the water bucket using the same water dipper. He recalls the rusty tin can hanging on the windmill for all to get a cold drink of well water. He can still see the brown gentle eyes of the first old milk cow he grew to love. He realized now how patient she was with him as he learned to milk. He remembers the light from the kerosene lamps he saw and did his homework for school with. His memories are fond of his parents, brothers and sisters. He still remembers his dad taking the time from a busy farm life to tell his son about the Arkansas Red Cedar Tree. Lonnie took the time to tell his children and grandchildren the story his dad told him. Now it is his children and grandchildren's turn to pass the story on.

Mrs. Hopper Visits Kindergarten

Written By
Lloyd Wright

Mrs. Hopper Visits Kindergarten

Mrs. Emma Hopper was sitting in her living room looking at her brightly lit Christmas tree. Christmas was over and the New Year was here. It was time to take her little Christmas tree down and pack it away for another year. She enjoyed it so much and it gave her a lot of satisfaction just having it shine in her window. She got up and while she was looking at the Christmas tree she saw the school bus coming down the street. She started waving and saw the children looking out of the school bus windows waving back. She stood there by the window waving until the bus was out of sight.

She made herself a cup of hot tea and sat down in her old squeaky rocking chair. The old chair had carried her on a trip down memory lane more times than she could count. As she rocked and listened to the chair's relaxing squeak, she thought about the school children that came and sang Christmas carols to her. As she closed her eyes, she could still see them as angels standing in her front yard singing. She opened her eyes and saw all the decorations the children had given her and the new string of lights on the tree. She remembered the two teachers visiting her and inviting her to come to school and visit their classes. She would love to see the children's bright shining faces again and hear their little voices. The squeak in the old rocker told her to take time and get out of the house and make good use of her life and to just not sit and rock her life away.

The next morning after she had eaten her breakfast of hot oatmeal, she took her cup of coffee and sat in her old rocker. She looked at the old clock on the wall and saw it was time for the school bus to be coming down the street. She sat her cup of coffee down and walked over by the front window. As she stood and watched for the bus, she turned on the Christmas tree lights for the last time this Holiday Season. The little tree must be taken down today and packed away again until the next Christmas Season is in the air. She heard the bus before she saw it. As soon as it was in sight she started waving. It made her feel happy inside to see the children's smiling faces in the bus window and all the children waving to her.

After the bus was out of sight she walked back to her rocking chair and started to let the familiar squeak carry her down memory lane, when she suddenly stopped rocking. She asked herself!

"Emma, just what are you doing still sitting here rocking your life away? Pick up that telephone and call the elementary school office. It won't hurt if the Christmas tree stays up and decorated for a while longer. It makes you happy and brightens up the living room."

Mrs. Hopper picked up the telephone book off of the stand next to her chair and looked for the telephone number of the school. After she found the number she called the elementary school office. A nice lady answered the phone and answered all the questions Mrs. Hopper asked her. When Mrs. Hopper hung up the receiver on the phone, she had a pleasant smile on her face. She was going to drive Old Herald to visit the children at school after lunch. She called her old pick up truck, Old Herald, because that is what her husband had called it when he was alive and they lived in the country. It needed some exercise anyway; she only drove it to church on Sunday and to the grocery store when she needed groceries. She couldn't afford to trade it for a car. Anyway, it held too many memories.

She hummed as she dusted her house and vacuumed the floors. She didn't feel like just sitting in her rocking chair; she had something to look forward to. She did not know what to expect, but she would find out. She made herself a bowl of hot vegetable soup and a sandwich for lunch. After she had eaten and washed the dishes, she put on the dress she always wore to church. She wanted to look nice for the children. She put on her good worn coat and then stood in front of the mirror and put on a hat. Ladies always wear a hat when they are going somewhere important.

Mrs. Hopper backed Old Herald out of the driveway and drove

slowly to the school. She followed the signs, which directed her to the elementary office. She could feel her heart beating faster, because she really did not know what to expect. She parked her truck and walked to the office and signed in as required of all visitors. One of the ladies in the office showed her where to go. She gently knocked on the door to the kindergarten classroom she wanted to visit first and slowly opened it. When she entered the room she saw the children sitting quietly as their teacher read them a story. The children immediately recognized Mrs. Hopper and wanted to get up out of their seats and give her a welcome hug but were not allowed to. Their teacher gave her a hug and welcomed Mrs. Hopper to the classroom.

Mrs. Hopper was introduced to each student again and was then asked if she would like to read a story to the children. Mrs. Hopper had never read to children before. The classroom had a rocking chair for the teacher and a mat for the children to sit on as a story was read. At first she started to refuse, but the children all wanted her to. She sat down in the rocking chair and began to rock ever so slowly. At first she was uneasy reading but as she read the story about a frog that could not jump she became as interested in the story as the children. When she had finished the story a little ruffled haired boy held up his hand. When asked by the teacher what he wanted he said.

"Can I ask Mrs. Hopper something?"

The teacher gave him her permission.

The little boy got up and walked up to Mrs. Hopper and leaned against her as he said.

"I don't have a grandmother and no one ever reads me a story at home. They are always too busy going somewhere. Will you be my grandmother and read to my class again?"

Mrs. Hopper knew at that very moment she would be a volunteer to read to the children. She was now a grandma to all the kindergarten children in that class. She stayed in the classroom for thirty minutes and then told the teacher she must visit the other kindergarten class who sang Christmas carols at her home. Before she could get up out of the rocking chair, each student came up to her and gave her a hug. The entire class wanted to call her Granny, which met her approval. She had never been a grandma before.

Two of the students escorted her to the other kindergarten classroom. She was met with the same enthusiasm by the teacher and the children. She also read the class a story about a bluebird with a sore beak. It had tried to eat the seeds from a wooden artificial flower. She enjoyed the story as much as the children. Her eyes kept wandering to a little girl with sad eyes. She wondered about the little girl's home life. The little girl touched her heart. She knew she had to visit this classroom again and find out more about this student. She did receive hugs from all the students in the class. They also wanted to know if she would read to their class again and if they could call her Granny. She said.

"I would be very happy to read to you and be called Granny."

Mrs. Hopper signed out from the school and walked to her old truck. After she started the engine, she just sat there for a while and watched the older students as they walked to different classrooms. She drove home slowly. When she arrived home, she made herself a hot cup of tea. She slowly rocked in her rocking chair and sipped the tea. She was tired, but it was a good feeling tired. She now had a family who called her Granny. She finished her tea and then let the squeak of her rocking chair lull her to sleep.

A Date To Remember

Written By
Lloyd Wright

A Date To Remember

Little Lonnie was nick named, "Question Box," when he was first old enough to asked questions. He continually peppered his dad with questions. If he ask.

"Can we go fishing dad?"

His dad knew they had fishing poles and were both healthy so he would reply.

"Sure we can go fishing."

When Lonnie discovered they were not going fishing right away, he then would ask.

"When are we going fishing dad?"

His dad would smile as he replied.

"We will go fishing October the eleventeenth."

Little Lonnie would then be satisfied because he now knew when they would be going fishing. He would leave his dad alone for awhile as he would go play. It would not be long before he thought about his friend and he would find his dad and ask.

"Dad can I ride my bicycle to see my friend Darrel?"

His dad knew there was a lot of traffic on the road his son would have to ride his little bicycle on, so he would reply.

"Lonnie, you are too young to be riding your bicycle on the road to see you friend. You must wait until you are older."

Lonnie would then ask.

"When will I be old enough Dad?"

His dad would smile and reply.

"You will be old enough when it is October eleventeenth."

Lonnie would be again be satisfied because he now knew when he would be old enough to ride his bicycle to visit his friend who lived down the road.

Lonnie was in the second grade before he discovered there was no October eleventh on the calendar. He found out quickly when he did not have his homework done and the teacher asked him.

"Lonnie when are you going to have the assignment done you were supposed to do as homework and turn in today?"

Lonnie squirmed in his seat and then replied loud and clear.

"I will have it done on October the eleventeenth."

That was the day he found out why he never went fishing or any other place that was supposed to happen on that date. Lonnie always remembered that special date. When he had children of his own he would satisfy their inquisitive minds with the same answer when they wanted to know, "when."

Lonnie did become a grandpa and had grandchildren who were question boxes. He always remembered his dad's answer and knew his dad was right. Sure you can as long as you are capable of doing something or going somewhere. So the answer to can we is; yes we can. The whole key to satisfying their little inquisitive minds in tell them exactly when. That answer is still October the elventeenth.

So to all parents of young children, just remember that all important date.

A Very Special Key

Written By
Lloyd Wright

A Very Special Key

Little Roger was walking home from school with his friends when he saw a reflection of something in the grass. He was curious as all young boys are and had to see what was lying in the grass. He walked over and saw a shiny key with a note attached to it with a red string. He picked the key up and showed it to his friends before he put it in his pocket. One friend wanted the key, but Roger would not part with it. When he arrived home safe and sound and was sitting at the kitchen table eating a peanut butter and jelly sandwich, he thought about the key he had found. He showed it to his mom. She looked at the key and then read the attached note to him.

"Whoever finds this key and can find the door it unlocks, they will be able to travel anywhere in the world free whenever they want to."

Roger did not understand what the note meant and neither did his mother. He did know he would carry the key with him where ever he went and try to open all doors. He first tried the key in the front door lock of their house. It did not fit, so he tried the back door lock. It also did not fit that lock either. He tried it on the locks to his dad's work shop with no luck. He showed the key to his dad when he came home from work. His dad didn't know what it meant but let his son try the key on the car door lock and ignition key hole.

Roger got on his bicycle and rode over to see his friend who lived just down the street. When he arrived he showed the key to his friend again who had wanted the key. They tried it on all the house locks at his friend's house. It never unlocked a single lock. They tried it on the work shop in his friend's backyard. They still had no luck. They rode their bicycles to their other friends they went to school with and tried the key in all their locks. The key was beginning to seem worthless to them or maybe it was someone trying to fool them. After they played baseball the rest of the afternoon, Roger took his key and went home.

He put it on the nightstand by his bed and as he looked at it, he thought about all the trips he would like to take and all the places he would like to see. He just could not imagine what the note on the key meant. If the key could take him anyplace in the world, then he knew he must keep trying. The key fascinated him so much he even dreamed about it that night. When he awoke the next morning, he had to look to see if the key was still on the stand. After he was dressed for the day, he put the key in his pocket. It was Saturday and his mom was going shopping today and he was going to go with her.

Roger's mother spent the morning going store to store shopping. Every store they went into Roger had to try his key in the door lock. When his mom would meet a friend and take time to visit between stores, Roger would try the key in all the store doors close by. The key didn't even come close to fitting any of the locks. He even tried the key in locks the store had on display racks. He was getting desperate. The next morning when he went to Sunday School and Church he tried his key in all the locks he could find. People would look at him and wonder what he was doing. His mom and dad had to explain to people who questioned them what he was doing and why.

Roger was tired from trying his key in every lock he could find or think of. He would not give up though. There are so many places in this world he wanted to visit and especially for free anytime he wanted to go visit them. On Monday, Roger walked to school with his friends. He showed all of them the special key as they hopped, skipped, and jumped their way to school. When he arrived at school he tried the key on the front door of the school. Needless to say it did not fit. He tried the key in every classroom door in the hallway until a teacher saw him and made him quit that foolishness. When he walked into his classroom, he showed the key to his teacher. She read the note attached with a red string to the special key. He told her he had tried the key in a million locks and none of them would open. She said.

"Roger, just keep trying and maybe you will find the door which has behind it all your free trips."

Roger carried the key in his pocket all of the next week to school. He still had not found the lock his key would open. While Roger was eating his breakfast Saturday morning, his mother said.

"Roger, you have a book checked out from the Public Library that needs turned in or they will fine you for an over due book."

After the breakfast dishes were done and the floor swept, Roger's mom made up her grocery list for the week. After they went to the library, they would do the grocery shopping. Roger found his library book on his dresser in his bedroom. Just then his mom said.

"Roger, I am ready to go down town; bring your book and come on."

The first stop was the City Public Library. When they pulled into the parking lot, they saw people lined up at the front door. As they approached the library, they saw the librarian looking in her purse. She could not find her key to the front door. Roger remembered his key and asked her if his would fit. She asked him where he got the key with the note. He told her where he had found it and how he tried to open a million locks. The key was shaped and notched like the front door key to the library. She said.

"Roger, you have tried the key on a million other locks; you may as well try the front door lock to the library."

Roger took his key and put it in the front door lock. It slid in easy. When he tried to turn the key it turned and unlocked the door. The librarian then said.

"Roger you can take your free trips now when you read the books in this library."

Mrs. Finch's Annual Christmas Program

WRITTEN BY
LLOYD WRIGHT

Mrs. Finch's Annual
Christmas Program

This program is about caring animals that can talk, an old barn and children. They all come together during a snowstorm on Mr. Jensen's farm showing love, caring and sharing.

Miracles In The Old Barn

1. (Sing) "Gramps Jensen had a farm."

Gramps Jensen had a farm, E-I-E-I-O
And on his farm he had a cow, E-I-E-I-O
With a moo-moo here, and a moo-moo there
Gramps Jensen had a farm, E-I-E-I-O

----he had a pig, with a oink-oink
----he had a horse, with a neigh-neigh
----he had a rabbit, with a twitch-twitch
----he had a mouse, with a squeak-squeak
----he had a dog, with a woof-woof
----he had a cat, with a meow-meow
----he had a skunk, with a peeeeee-youuuuuu

(Gramps) Farmer Jensen had just finished the chores and decided to turn the animals out into the pasture. As they walked into the pasture, Bessie, the Holstein cow said, "It feels like a storm is in the air." Jessaline the Jersey cow quickly agreed. Bill the sorrel and Ben the Bay were old but feeling spry and they galloped to the back of the pasture by the old barn. They were out of breath!

136

2. (Sing) "Christmas Cowboys."

(Gramps) After they got their breath, the horses talked about the barn and how it was full of alfalfa hay and grain they had helped farmer Jensen haul there. They both agreed they could feel a change in the weather. The pigs and sheep just meandered around that morning. Charlene the cat was looking for a mouse to feed to her kittens that were hidden up in the hayloft. The animals heard the school bus go by to pick up the children. They knew Mr. Green was the bus driver. He had visited the farm quite often. Mr. Green could feel a chill in the air as the children were getting on the bus for the last day of school before Christmas. He noticed clouds gathering in the west. The children were all laughing and in a holiday kind of spirit as the bus bounced down the country road.

3. (Sing) "The Wheels on the Bus."

4. (Sing) "Jingle Bells."

5. (Sing) "Oh Christmas Tree."

6. (Sing) "Christmas is such a Happy time."

(Gramps) The sky was overcast by the time the bus arrived at school. Within one hour, the wind started blowing and snow was falling. When it was time for lunch, the ground was white and little drifts were forming. Anxious parents were calling the school office. School was let out early because of the storm. Mr. Green fought the snow choked roads trying to get the children home. Many times he had to back up and take a run at the snow drifts. The Christmas spirit prevailed as they tried to drive down the snow drifted road.

7. (Sing) "Let it Snow."

8. Sing "Go tell it on the Mountain.

(Gramps) When it started to snow hard, the horses started walking to the old barn. The cows followed since they were so far from the barnyard. All the animals were soon cozy in the old barn. The aroma of the alfalfa hay filled the barn as the storm raged outside.

9. (Sing) "Do you see what I see?"

(Gramps) The animals started talking since no one else was around. They remembered when Santa had stopped at the old barn when two of his reindeer were sick. He left the reindeer in the warm barn and Bill and Ben had volunteered to help Santa, but did not think they could fly. Santa asked them, if they believed in reindeer, toys, love, family and what happened in Bethlehem. They had seen the star in the east. Yes, they believed. Santa said. "Then you can fly."

10. (Sing) "Rudolph."

(Gramps) Up, up and away you horses and deer. The horses helped Santa that night and he granted them their wish that all animals could talk to each other. All the animals talked from that night on. Bessie started humming a Christmas carol and all the animals joined in.

11. (Sing) "Silent Night."

12. (Sing) "Joy to the World."

(Gramps) After going by the cross-fence on farmer Jensen's farm, the school bus got stuck in a huge snowdrift. A blizzard was raging and it had caused a whiteout. The bus was about out of gas, so Mr. Green had all the children hang onto each other in a single file, as he led them following the fence to the old barn. The children thought they heard Christmas carols but when they reached the old barn all they found was animals. The children were very cold and on the verge of frost bite. Bessie and Jessaline had the pigs pile up straw for the children. After the children were in the straw, the sheep let the children put their hands in their wool and lay on their feet to get the children warm. Bill and Ben got the saddles blankets and burlap sacks to cover the children. A voice told Mr. Green to milk Jessaline and give the children the warm rich milk. He then milked Bessie as told. Roy the rooster sat on his perch above watching. All the animals reminded him of farmer Jensen, as they shared, gave love and expected nothing in return.

13. (Sing) "My favorite Things."
(Repeat song two times)

(Gramps) Shep was in the new barn waiting for his friends. He decided he had better go look for them. When he found them in the old barn, Bessie asked him if he would lead Ben to the farm house and get farmer Jensen to help the children. Shep led Ben through the blinding snowstorm and then told farmer Jensen they could talk and the children needed his help. He never knew they could talk. He got several thermos jugs of soup and warm blankets and returned to the old barn with Ben and Shep. He told Mrs. Jensen he would stay with the children until the storm quit.

14. (Sing) "What did you say was the Baby's Name?"

(Gramps) After the children were warm and fed, Bessie started humming a Christmas carol.

15. (Sing) "Away in the Manger."

(Gramps) The next morning found the storm gone. Farmer Jensen harnessed Bill and Ben to an old horse drawn sleigh he had in the north end of the barn. He took the children to his house, where Granny Jensen gave each one a hug and a huge breakfast. After breakfast, they rode in the old sleigh to their homes as they sang Christmas carols all the way. The children at times thought they were flying. Bill and Ben winked at each other when they heard the children talk about flying. Mr. Green still is not sure about hearing the animals talk and sing.

16. (Sing) "The Peppermint Stick Song."

17. (Sing) "Happy Birthday Jesus."

18. (Sing) "We wish you a Merry Christmas."

(Children take a bow)

When The Spring Flowers Bloom

Written By
Lloyd Wright

When The Spring Flowers Bloom

Tracy was excited over her trip tomorrow to visit Grandmother Ellie and had a hard time going to sleep. She closed her eyes and thought about her past visits. Every summer since she was two years old she had stayed at Grandmother's house for two weeks. Grandmother Ellie lived a long way away and she only got to visit with her twice a year. She saw grandmother during her visits every summer and in the spring her grandmother would come to her house for a visit. Her mom and dad would drive to Grandmother Ellie's house and stay overnight and then leave to go back home. They would take the same trip when Tracy's two week visit was over.

She loved to stay at Grandmother's house. She had kind of an old house, but it was filled with so many interesting things. She always got to sleep with Grandmother Ellie in her big fluffy bed. Grandmother Ellie let her help cook and bake and best of all, she helped her in the flower garden. Grandmother Ellie loved to work in her backyard and watch her flowers grow and reward her with their beauty when they bloomed. She also had a bird feeder and let her help feed the birds and then they would sit on the porch swing and watch the birds eat. When the birds sang Grandmother Ellie would say.

"Listen to the birds sing Tracy. They are thanking us for the food and water."

Grandmother also has an old hunting dog that had been Grandpa's dog before he went away to a special place for nice Grandpas. Grandpa had named him, "Tracker," but she re-named him, Yawner," because he spends most of his day lying by the back kitchen door and if he hears a noise will open one eye and yawn, stretch and then go back to snoozing. She said.

"He is a good guard dog. If anyone wants in the back door he will look with one eye and yawn and then make them trip over him, because he is too lazy to move out of the way. He thinks the rug on the back porch by the kitchen door is his bed."

He knows to stay out of her flower garden, too. Grandmother told her she broom trained him. She had never heard of broom training and never knew what it meant until Grandmother Ellie said.

"When he would get in my flower beds I would get my old straw kitchen broom and whack him. It only took a few times and then he knew to stay out of the flowers. He does like to smell them from the edge of the flower beds; you know hunting dogs are good smellers."

Tracy finally fell off to sleep and dreamland. She did wake up early and ran down stairs to make sure her parents were awake; today they were going to Grandmother Ellie's house. She found her dad sitting at the kitchen table drinking a cup of coffee and her mom was fixing breakfast. Tracy's mom said.

"Good morning Tracy; today you get to go see Grandmother Ellie's. You have time to wash your hands and face and get dressed before breakfast is ready."

Tracy scurried upstairs and proceeded to wash and then put on her clothes for the trip. She was anxious to see her grandmother. She had a lot of things planned during her visit. She was going to be sixteen soon and had a driver's learner permit; maybe Grandmother would let her drive the car when they went somewhere. She did live in a very small town. It had a main street and a city square in the center of town and that was just about it. It was a small farming community. Before school was out for the summer, she had told her sophomore English teacher all about her grandmother Ellie and all the fun they would have together this summer. Tracy had packed her suitcase and repacked it a dozen times. She had not seen her grandmother since she had come to visit for a week during the spring. She liked to visit when the spring flowers were blooming. She would take her granddaughter Tracy's hand and together examine and smell all the flowers. She especially loved to look inside a tulip's bloom and would admire its beauty. She always said to Tracy.

"When the spring flowers bloom they are telling us the winter is over and it is time for all the birds and animals to start a family. It is the time to re-new life and also time to prepare the ground for planting."

Tracy could still see the sparkle in her grandmother's eyes and the joy written all over her face as she inspected the tulips, daffodils and crocus. Tracy's mom had said.

"Grandmother Ellie's favorite time of year when I was a little girl was when the spring flowers bloomed. She used to take me by the hand like she does yours, and we would look at the spring flowers together."

After breakfast, they loaded the suitcases in the car and were soon on their way to Grandmother's house. Tracy did ask her dad if she could drive part of the way and received the answer she knew she would hear. Tracy knew it would be dangerous on a busy highway for her to drive but she had to ask anyway. The trip lasted four hours, which seemed like an eternity to Tracy. When they finally arrived at their destination they found Grandmother Ellie sitting on the front porch swing anxiously waiting. Tracy leaped out of the car as soon as she could and ran to her Grandmother's waiting arms. Her dad and mom walked onto the porch and they also received a big welcoming hug. As her dad hugged Grandmother he said.

"Something sure smells good."

Grandmother replied.

"Come on in the house, I have dinner waiting for you. I knew you would be hungry."

When they went into the house they found a dinner of roast beef, mashed potatoes, gravy, creamed green peas fresh from the garden, roasting ears and an apple pie still hot from the oven. After the meal was through and the dessert with ice cream eaten, Tracy and her mother wanted to do the dishes while Grandmother Ellie rested. She would have none of that and pitched right in. Tracy's dad unloaded the suitcases from the car while the dishes were being done. During the afternoon, Tracy's dad sat on the back porch swing and watched the three girls in his life walking in the backyard chatting and looking at flowers. The evening meal consisted of left over roast beef with the left over trimmings, much to the disappointment of old Yawner. He did stick his nose close to the kitchen screen door and take in all the aroma which passed through the screen. When the evening meal was over, Yawner was pleased to find they had not eaten all the huge meal he had smelled cooking that morning.

In the cool of the evening, they all sat on the back porch and took in the sounds of nature. Tracy loved to hear the squeak of Grandmother's old wooden rocking chair as she gentle rocked. When she was younger, she would be on her Grandmother's lap listening to the squeak along with Grandmother's heart beat. They all made a wish on the first star they saw shining down on them. The summer, golden moon even seemed to shine brighter at Grandmother's house. It was bedtime too soon. Tracy did not even have to ask where she would be sleeping. She knew she would be in Grandmother's big soft bed just like all the years before.

Grandmother Ellie was up early and had coffee made and breakfast cooking on the stove by the time Tracy woke up. It was the smell of sausage and toast in the air that greeted her the next morning. She dressed quickly and when she walked into the kitchen, her parents were already up and having a cup of coffee. Tracy had to give her grandmother a hug right away. She was so glad to be with her again. After a hearty breakfast and the breakfast dishes washed and put away, Tracy's parents bid good-by and started their journey back home.

Grandmother Ellie had a days work to do with her granddaughter. Today they would pick beans and roasting ears from the garden. When they had the harvest on the back porch, they sat on the swing and visited as they kept their hands busy snapping beans to can and shucking corn to put in the freezer. Tracy did not mind the work at all, in fact it was not work as long as she could visit and learn. They had a noon meal of roasting ears, fresh green beans and fried chicken. They finished canning the beans and putting the corn in the freezer after lunch. When they were through, they strolled in the back yard looking at the flowers and watered those, which needed it. When the sun was in the west, they put grain in the bird feeders and then sat on the back porch swing and watched and listened to the birds.

They ate a sandwich and fruit for the evening meal. When they were through for the day, they walked in the front yard and Grandmother Ellie showed Tracy where all the spring flowers were planted. Most of them were now hidden until it was time to spread their cheer again in late winter and early spring. They took time to smell the rose bushes in full bloom. It was a nice evening and perfect to sit on the porch and swing which they did until the stars came out and the moon showed its bright face. Tracy laid her head on her grandmother's shoulder and Grandmother put her arm around her and ever so gently hugged her. Neither one had to tell the other the love they felt for each other.

The next morning, Grandmother Ellie showed Tracy how to bake bread and cinnamon rolls. For lunch they had fresh bread with some of Grandmother's homemade jelly. Tracy had a glass of milk and a hot cinnamon roll. After they had toured the flower beds, Grandmother opened the garage doors and said.

"Tracy, I think it is time you take your old Grandma for a ride in the country."

Tracy was very excited. Grandmother Ellie started the car and backed it out of the garage and turned it around in the driveway. She got out and handed Tracy the keys. She lived by the edge of the small town and they were soon enjoying the sights of the countryside. For the next two hours they chatted and looked as they slowly drove down country roads. They even stopped and visited with one of Grandmother's friends and had tea and cookies. Grandmother Ellie was so very proud to introduce her granddaughter to her friend. When they finally arrived back at Grandmother's house, they fed and watered the birds and then slowly swung together as they watched and listened. After a bowl of soup, sandwich and a piece of pie for dessert, they sat on the front porch and listened to the sounds of Mother Nature as she changed from light to darkness.

Tracy enjoyed her visit everyday and everyday her grandmother would show or teach her something new. On Sunday, Tracy got to drive her grandmother to church. It was hard to tell by the looks on their face which one was prouder of each other. As they were getting ready to go to church, Grandmother gave Ellie a small silk handkerchief and said.

"When I was your age, every young lady had a silk handkerchief to carry to church. Your grandpa bought this handkerchief for me when your mother was born."

Grandmother carried a covered dish to church, because after the church service the congregation was having a pot luck dinner. This really gave Grandmother Ellie a chance to introduce and show off Tracy. It was mid-afternoon when they arrived home. It was time to swing and enjoy the back yard view and smell the fragrance of the flowers blooming. It was that afternoon as they sat on the swing Grandmother Ellie said.

"Tracy, we only get to see each other twice a year. I wish I lived closer to you. When I am too old and feeble to travel to visit you in the spring, I will still be with you when you see the spring flowers bloom."

The next week Tracy was kept busy as she helped hoe and water the garden, tend the flowers and help can the abundant garden vegetables. They baked cookies, pies and cakes. Grandmother had taught her a lot when it came to cooking. Tracy would help her mother more in the kitchen after this visit. Some nights they opened the windows to the bedroom and as they lay in the big soft bed, listened to the night sounds. The chirp of a cricket is so peaceful at night. After a rain, the frogs would join together in chorus. Sometime they would hear Yawner make his rounds to check to see if all was well in the back yard. Then they would hear his toenails click on the wooden back porch as he walked over to the backdoor and his bed.

Tracy's parents came as planned to get Tracy. They spent the afternoon visiting with Grandmother and catching up on the news. Tracy hated to go to bed that night. She knew the night would pass too quickly and she would have to leave. Grandmother Ellie and Tracy did lay awake a long time softly talking. Tracy lay next to her grandmother and did shed a tear. Dawn did appear before she was ready for it. After a hearty breakfast, it was time to load the suitcases and go home. Tracy kissed and hugged Grandmother Ellie. Both of them were shedding tears. Grandmother Ellie wiped Tracy's tears as she said.

"I will see you when the spring flowers bloom sweetheart."

Grandmother Ellie unexpectedly went to see Grandpa just as a single hearty daffodil pushed through the snow and opened its' bloom. When Tracy stood and looked at the hearty little flower through tears, she knew Grandmother Ellie was there with her and would be every spring.

Johnny Is Going Nowhere

Written By
Lloyd Wright

Johnny Is Going Nowhere

Little Johnny straps on his gun belt and puts his toy revolver in the holster. He picks up his cowboy hat and put it on and is running toward the back door when his mom asks.

"Where are you going so fast?"

Johnny answers without stopping.

"Nowhere mom."

Johnny runs outside and into the backyard. He has his horse waiting for him to ride to uphold the law of the land. His horse is one of his dad's sawhorses. The new leather bridle with silver buckles is a rope he found in his dad's workshop. The new saddle is the rug off of the back porch. He unties his horse as he says.

"Easy Thunder, it is time we head to the hills and catch those outlaws that robbed the bank."

Johnny eased up into the saddle and as he held the reins loosely he said.

"Giddyup Thunder."

He reins Thunder to the west toward the nearby hills. He picks up the outlaws' trail quickly. He can tell by their horse's tracks they are traveling fast to get as much distance between them and the law as they can. What they didn't know was his horse, Thunder, was the fastest horse in the territory. Ever so often, he would have to dismount and look closely to pick up their trail in the rocky terrain. After he had trailed them for a long time, he saw their campfire smoke in the distance. He dismounted and tied Thunder to a tree. He ran into the house to get a drink and something to eat. When he walked in the back door his mom asked.

"Where have you been Johnny?"

Johnny replied.

"Nowhere, can I have a glass of milk and some cookies?"

His mom replied.

"You sure can cowboy after you wash your hands."

Little Johnny washed his hands in the nearby mountain stream in the bathroom. When he returned to the campsite in the kitchen, he found a glass of milk and three cookies on the table. His mother sat down at the table with him and took her midmorning break. As soon as the last cookie disappeared, he put on his cowboy hat and headed toward the back door.

His mom said.

"Hold on there cowboy; where are you going so fast?"

As Johnny opened the door he said.

"Nowhere."

Thunder was waiting patiently as he swished his tail to keep flies away. Johnny untied him from the tree and mounted up. He double checked his toy gun and turned Thunder toward the outlaw's campfire. He had to cross two mountain streams and climb one high mountain. He surprised the outlaws and after a long gun battle he captured all of them. He took them to town and turned them over to the sheriff. He did receive the bounty on them.

After he arrived back home, he unsaddled Thunder and climbed up into the big oak tree by his dad's workshop. He had a favorite branch half way up the tree he sat on and rode the wind. He could see for miles sitting on the branch, as the wind gently swayed the branch back and forth. Finally, he decided to climb to the top and fly around the world. A squirrel scolded him as he climbed up into its' territory. He watched as it gave up and jumped to another tree. He was now king of the land. He could see for miles as he flew the treetop like an airplane. He traveled to places he had heard his teacher talk about. As he flew over the countryside, he saw farmers working in their fields and people fishing from big boats in lakes. He saw mountains that hid their tops in the clouds. He guided his airplane around them.

He finally landed the airplane and climbed down from the tree. He took the rug he used for a saddle and laid on it as he watched the white fluffy clouds floating lazily in the blue sky. He could see all different kinds of shapes as the clouds floated by. He saw lions, horse, castles and faces of people. He picked out a big fluffy looking cloud and let his mind drift. He was soon riding the cloud as it gently drifted in the sky. He rode it around the world and even visited storybook land. He visited castles, kings and queens. The cloud was his chariot as he rode through the heavens. He heard somebody calling his name from a nearby cloud. He listened closely as it said.

"Johnny, stop your daydreaming and come into the house and wash for dinner."

Johnny opened his eyes and found he had landed back into his own backyard after riding the big, white, fluffy cloud. When he walked into the house his mom asked.

"Where have you been son?"

Johnny replied.

"Nowhere mom."

Johnny washed his hands and face and was then ready to eat. He was hungry as a bear after his morning travels. He had heard his dad say sometimes.

"I am hungry enough to eat fried rocks!"

Johnny decided he was hungry enough to eat fried rocks also.

He soon discovered he did not have to because his mom had fixed him a big bowl of his favorite soup and a hamburger. He ate a piece of cake and a dish of jell-O for dessert. After eating lunch his mom made him lie down and rest for a while. As he lay on the couch in the living room, his mind took him to far away places. He was riding in a space ship and could even see more than he did flying the treetop or riding the cloud. His imagination was so peaceful he fell asleep, as he traveled nowhere.

When Little Johnny woke up from a short nap, he started to go outside when his mom asked him.

"Where are you going?"

As the back screen door slammed shut, she heard him answer.

"Nowhere mom."

Johnny decided to get his bicycle out of the garage and ride it over to his grandpa's house, but he knew he couldn't so he just pretended.

He imagined his bicycle was a motorcycle and did a wheelie as he left burnt rubber on the driveway. He took some of the reward money for capturing the bank robbers and stopped at the ice cream store. He could just imagine what it would be like to be in an ice cream store and eat all the ice cream you wanted. He even bought some for his grandma and grandpa. He rode so fast it didn't even melt. He stayed at his grandparent's house long enough to eat some more ice cream and fresh home made cookies Grandma had just taken out of the oven.

Just thinking about ice cream and cookies made him hungry. He parked his motorcycle bicycle with out even leaving the driveway. He rode all over town but never went anywhere. When he ran into the house he asked.

"Mom, can I have some ice cream and cookies?"

His mom had been baking cookies and she knew he had smelled them while he rode his bicycle on the driveway. She replied.

"Wash your hands and face and I'll scoop you some ice cream to go with your cookies. By the way, where have you been?"

Little Johnny said.

"Nowhere."

After Little Johnny had finished his afternoon snack, he again headed for the back door. His mom asked him.

"Where are you going Johnny boy?"

Johnny answered without even stopping.

"Nowhere mom."

Johnny spent the rest of the afternoon traveling with the circus as he did his stunts on his swing and jungle gym.

When his dad got home from work he yelled.

"Hi Johnny, come on in the house. Your mother has supper on the table."

When Johnny was eating supper with his family, his dad said.

"Where have you been today?"

Johnny said.

"Oh, I have been nowhere today dad."

When Johnny's mom tucked him in bed that night she said.

"You sure are a tired young man for having gone nowhere all day!"